Also by Keith Nixon

<u>Konstantin Series</u>
The Fix
Dream Land
Russian Roulette

<u>Caradoc Series</u>
The Eagle's Shadow
The Eagle's Blood

<u>Standalone novel</u>
The Corpse Role

Author's Note

Today

I'm lucky to be sitting at my laptop, with you looking over my shoulder. Should be on a beach somewhere, unwinding, but instead I'm here because the story is far too big to suppress, like an elephant in a paper bag. So I must write it. Before they come for me. Kill it forever.

However, my fingers linger over the keys. I hesitate to force even a letter to appear on the screen because I really don't want to go over it all again. The first time was bad enough. In fact it was the worst time.

All that fear, death and mayhem, expecting to make it through to the end in several pieces.

In the last five days everyone has been after my head:

The gangsters.
The terrorists.
And worst of all – the police. The copper at the middle of the spider's web, pulling all the strings but just part of a wider, deeper conspiracy.

Finally, I get up the nerve; my fingertips start to rattle at the keys like rain on a windowpane.
It all began with a dead man...

Prologue
A Maximum High

A Year Ago

The building stands head and shoulders above its neighbours. An imposing, grey façade, perfected over hundreds of years to intimidate and control the flock. There, at its dizzying peak, someone steps up onto the crenelated edge, peers downward, unaffected by the sheer precipice.

The jumper glimpses gargoyles clinging onto the tower. Giggles at the irony. Designed to keep evil away, yet suicide is itself a sin. Ah, the black humour of the situation.

It would be so easy, so very, very easy for the jumper to close their eyes and blot out the magnificent view. Drop off and feel like a bird in flight. Like the dream from childhood. But there would be no waking up from this slumber.

However, the jumper isn't ready, hasn't quite made peace with the world. Just needs a few more moments. Until it feels utterly right.

A scrunch of gravel intrudes. A footfall, an interloper not quite cautious enough. Behind. Close by. The jumper turns. Sees men.

"You don't have to do this," one says.

"Leave me alone!" Desperation grips every syllable. "Just let me go!"

Now that there's nothing to live for.

The jumper looks forward, spreads arms out like an angel dressed in black, lifts shuttered eyes to the heavens. Whispers a prayer. A slow lean forward…

Gone.

But a hand clutches the jumper's clothes, bunches them together in a firm grip that's not letting go. The jumper struggles, but more hands enclose arms, ankles. Lift and pull.

The jumper hits the ground, face scrapes on the gravel, breath punches out of lungs. Screws eyes shut, remembers the vista, enjoys the pain. Registers the kiss of cold steel and the sound of a ratchet, as cuffs close over wrists.

Begins to scream and never stops.

The U-Bend of Life

Five Days Ago

If I'm honest, I'm really not in the mood, not in the fucking slightest. I'm so tired.

Not because I haven't slept adequately (three hours partially interrupted). Not because I've a hangover (only four cans of lager and a half bottle of Polish vodka, which is bugger all). Not because of excessive exercise (I revel in my lack of fitness).

No.

What weighs on me is the blackest of moods. I'm so worn; I've a rut six inches deep through my day. And I've only been out of bed for two minutes.

You find me in my mouldy bathroom, gingerly perching on frigid porcelain. The boxers I've barely slept in crowd my ankles, blind eye turned to the stains within. I'm avoiding undertaking several activities:

> Having a shower, because I can't be arsed turning on the taps.
> Scrubbing my teeth, as that would mean wetting a toothbrush, applying pressure to squeeze paste onto the bristles, energy to raise arm up horizontally to gums and a repetitive forth and back motion to scour off the food particles, germs and the beginnings of a plaque colony.
> Brushing hair, but it's a thatch. Pointless.

Ultimately, I cannot be bothered. So fuck it if I smell. I don't care if I need dentures in the future. Utterly apathetic to my appearance, because no-one is interested in me. Not anymore, anyway. I'm a shambles.

Facing me is a large bowl, atop a dwarf-sized table. Within, a jumble of items, mainly kids' toys, which my estranged wife used to drop into the bathwater to keep the offspring amused whilst they went through the ritual, and unwelcome, cleansing of the sole.

However, they became a low-profile casualty in the rush to dump Daddy. Since this meaningful event, the toys (not my kids) have developed interesting throngs of single-celled life, about as intelligent as me. Although of infinitely more value to the world.

But, in their midst, I spy with my little eye a bottle filled with green. Mouthwash.

Minimal expenditure of calories to grab it, twist off the cap, pour some into my throat straight from the bottle, swill and spit into the sink to my immediate left. Job done, teeth clean.

Thankfully, I don't need to wipe my arse. I couldn't manage it. So I stand, economically hiking up my boxers in the same movement.

I reason the problem is a gaping hole in my life. Several of them, actually.

You know about the family. I'm all on my lonesome. Restraining order still in place. Bitch.

There's also the job, or what's left of it. These days I'm pliable. Mr Do-What-I'm-Told-To. In the recent past, I could have replied with an "Up yours", because I'd been someone. But not anymore.

Now I have to take it, do it, be it. That's freelancing for you. That and losing your job in unsavoury circumstances, followed in short order by dignity, family, home, savings. And almost my life.

I step out of the bathroom; take the short trip across the hall to my bedroom. Begin to dress. Ask myself:

Why is life so unfair? I slowly button my shirt which is, in fact, missing a button.

Where did it all go wrong? I tuck myself in haphazardly. Modicum of difficulty doing up the trousers. Hands are shaking.

Where has it all gone? I tug on socks of a slightly different shade of black, but who gives a fuck? No-one looks at them anyway.

Then the phone rings. It seems like absolutely nothing, although the momentous occasions always do. Word of advice from the black-eyed wise; just don't say that to the wife on your wedding day.

Eventually, I realise this is what changes my life. But right now my gloom is too heavy for me to lift my head and see anything else going on around me.

"Hello? Yes, this is David Brodie speaking."

You. Idiot.

A Little Death In The Family

"I understand you can put me in touch with Mr Lamb," said Emily Hollowman, trying extremely hard not to breathe in through her nose lest she imbibe a dose of noxious body odour.

The object she addressed was a tramp, situated exactly where she'd been told to find him, on a strip of shit-strewn grass adjacent to the train station. He towered over her, despite her heels.

"Josh told me you'd be like this, that you wouldn't talk to me," Emily said.

The tramp maintained the impassive stance. Perhaps gave a slight shrug of a shoulder. It was hard to tell. He switched to bored. Yawned, glanced away, watched a car drive past with its exhaust rattling.

Emily decided to cut the crap, said, "Give him this please." Held out a piece of paper, jagged edges, phone number neatly written in red ink on the border. The tramp stretched out a paw and accepted the offering. It disappeared into his expansive palm.

They stood statue-like until Emily shook her head, turned and walked away.

So she didn't observe the tramp pull out his phone, make a call.

Konstantin Boryakov thrust grimy hands into grimier pockets and turned his back on Buenos Ayres to start the walk back into Margate. A brief lope brought the tramp into the looming shadow of Arlington House, a grim tower block built in the 1960s that appeared hewn out of seagull shit stained granite.

To all intents, he was invisible to the locals, but Konstantin knew it was mere pretence. Could see the trepidation in their eyes and the change in gait as he shambled towards them. But it was what he wanted. To be left alone. Particularly now.

His affable pace was enforced. Inside, Konstantin was in turmoil. James, dead. And in such dubious circumstances. It didn't make sense. Not that Konstantin had much liked James. They'd not even officially met, but that wasn't the point. It was that life was going to get that little bit harder for those he'd left behind.

It took fifteen minutes for the Russian to reach home – a narrow avenue of ramshackle, run-down terraced houses. All of which he owned, only one he occupied. Boarded up, they had the appearance of dereliction.

Konstantin entered the alley which ran directly behind the residences. It was full of discarded junk, half-chewed rubbish bags and rats. He paused. Looked one way, then the other. No one was within sight. He placed a grey, non-descript card against the graffiti strewn gate. Heard a click as the deadbolts demagnetised, pushed a shoulder against wood that was a lot more solid than it looked. Shut it behind him.

Into a covered walkway, lights flickered on along its length, casting their tungsten hue. High brick walls ran either side of him, a roof mere inches above his head. Muffled barking as the dogs did what they were trained to do. Another door, more locks, and he was inside.

Konstantin literally peeled off his heavily stained greatcoat, hung it on a sturdy hook adjacent the entrance. Thick and incredibly warm, it had once saved Konstantin when a mission in the fading stages of the Cold War had gone badly wrong. Muskö, just south of Stockholm.

Dripping wet and literally freezing to death, Konstantin happened across an airman. Took what he needed to survive, but at the cost of the airman's life. Once returned from the assignment, Konstantin folded up the coat, blood stains and all. Stuffed it into a box, it not seeing the light of day again until he'd escaped to the UK.

Boots followed coat as did, literally on their heels, the stench of clammy socks. He'd long ago stopped washing regularly and there was no-one else in the house to complain about the olfactory shortcoming this ultimately delivered.

Konstantin headed straight to the study, fired up a powerful PC and, whilst the software was kicking in, produced a significantly more authoritative coffee than Costa or Starbucks could possibly provide.

Turkish. Black, gritty and strong enough to take the enamel off your teeth.

When he returned, the computer was humming and the screensaver active. Konstantin nudged the mouse, cracked his knuckles and began to search. Although during the phone call Mr Lamb had given assurances that Superintendent Meadows would provide detailed information, the Russian preferred not to rely on others. He was a man short on trust.

By the time the dense coffee was down to the dregs, he'd found the beginnings of a structure. At the press of a button, the printer spewed out several pages of text. Konstantin gathered them up and slid them into a file.

He'd send Mr Lamb a text soon; give him the lowdown on what he knew. The man was a processor. Data went in, information was spat out. But it took time. It took patience too. And Konstantin had neither.

Instead, he closed the browser and opened up the word processing software. Konstantin was at the beginning of a long road, writing the wrongs in his memoirs. Perhaps today it was time to spell out the episode of the Swedish airman …

Lucy was primed and ready to burst. A man was following her and she knew exactly what to do. She just hoped to fuck he did.

She'd first heard his footsteps on entering the alleyway, a mimicking echo, slightly out of time with the click-clack of her high heels. She stole a fleeting glance over her shoulder. All she really detected was bulk – width, height. And anonymity, because his face was shrouded by a hood.

Lucy shivered with anticipation ... and slowed her pace slightly.

At the alley's conclusion, a right angle turn led her to a footbridge over railway tracks. She picked her way slowly upwards, the crumbling steps dangerous at most times of the year, but potential killers in the winter when they were slick with precipitation and rotting leaves. But combined with ridiculous heels?

Downright suicidal.

As she reached the midpoint of the overpass, the guy caught up with her. Lucy could hear his strangled wheezing. His weight made the bridge spring slightly. She stopped cold, twisted her body towards him, allowed her coat to flap open, revealing a short skirt and filmy top. Summer, not winter wear.

"Excuse me, love," he said as he squeezed by. "Hope I didn't worry you."

"No," Lucy replied with a microscopic, but inviting grin.

He returned the smile in lesser measure. Carried on. In a moment, he was descending and departing her troubled little world.

"*Fuck*," Lucy said under her breath. She stretched the word out, disappointment dripping through the four letters because she really needed one.

Was desperate for one. Just one little scuffle. She didn't care who with. Needed an adrenaline buzz. For old time's sake. But no-one wanted to play nasty.

She sighed, buttoned up her coat, then clattered carelessly down the steps. She couldn't care less if she slipped, fell, smashed her head in. Why should she? No-one else did.

But she was shit out of luck. Lucy made it down to the bottom in one chronically disappointed piece.

A Blast From The Past

It takes me three attempts to slam the door shut on my beat-up lump of metal that was originally a car. It should have retired disgracefully years ago.

The seat has the crevices worn in as proof, and there are stains on the once-beige upholstery I don't even want to consider the origins of. The mileage has been around the clock several times, not that it registers anymore, because the electrics are screwed. Which means the heating is shot. A bit of a problem in the depths of winter. But then the windscreen wipers, indicators and lights are also terminal.

C'est la vie, my friend.

Scooby Doo has the Mystery Machine, well I've got the Shit Machine. The dog's life was one long exciting series of intrigue and thrills, whereas mine is one long stream of … well, you get my drift.

At one time, I'd possessed a decent motor, but the ex-missus had away the people-carrier on account of needing to transport our little individuals, originally born out of love and now raised in antipathy.

I scratch at my chin, realise I've neglected to shave. Shrug. Who gives a shit? I'm my own boss. No-one looks at a reporter's face anyway.

Did I put on deodorant? Can't remember. A sniff of the pits leads me to the conclusion it probably went on one and certainly didn't on the other. So I decide its best not to get close to anyone today.

The thing with keeping ablutions down to a minimum? It's a haphazard affair, albeit far less time-consuming.

I wind the window down (yes, wind, the car is *that* prehistoric) and spark up a fag. I really shouldn't, petrol fumes saturate the interior. But that's something you should know about me early on in our relationship.

I don't care if I die.

This outlook, however, provides me with a fairly unique perception of life's rules (my shrink has tried unsuccessfully to prove otherwise). My latest pastime is ignoring traffic lights, just to see whether anyone or anything will hit me and put me out of my miserable misery. So far without success.

If nothing devastating happens soon, I'll have to select another 'accidental' self-harming process.

I shift my arse to get comfortable. There's a sound like Zebedee as a spring pings. Shove the key in ignition, multiple attempts to start the engine, car into gear. Phone rings.

Bastard, the phone's ringing. Get it or ignore it? I can't remember the last time I had two calls in a week, never mind a day.

Well, self-employed losers don't really get a choice, do they? I leave it to go to voicemail and cross my fingers that it's not the wife's solicitors. Or that shit I owe money to.

I leave the engine running. If I turn it off, it may never ignite again. Or I may gas myself to death as a result of a rusted-to-shit exhaust. Either way, everyone's a winner.

I wait. It's fucking cold. Say, "What do you want? Busy bastard on the go here." Lots of talking underway. Toes crossed now too.

Beep to say a text has come in. At last. "You've got voicemail," it says. I dial the number, knowing this is at my cost, when originally they called me. Better safe than sorry, though.

"Hello? Dave? You there? Have I got the wrong number then?" the recording says. Slightly effeminate, hairdresser type tone, vague Welsh accent. Gray it is then. And he doesn't seem to have a clue he's talking to a machine, not David Brodie.

"Yeah, I'm here," I reply to no-one but myself and the phone.

I take a draw on my fag, realise I'm down to the butt. I bin it out the window. Disgusting habit, shortens your life span (good). But maybe it will land in a stream of petrol and ...

Gray laughs in my ear. "Only joking!"

"Get on with it, mate."

"I've got something for you ..."

"I seriously doubt it. What can I do for you? Busy boy and all that?"

"... No, but you'll like this one. You know that girl, Lucy, the one I've been telling you about?"

Unfortunately, I do. Gray has been trying to fix me up ever since the missus cleared off. He has this misguided belief that meeting another woman will help a broken-hearted man recover all the faster. What crap. Relationships are trouble. Why would I want another?

"Uh-huh," I say, drifting.

"... Well, I'm meeting her soon. On your behalf, of course ..."

I groan.

"... Frankly she can be a bit of a nutter ..."

This revelation isn't really helping convince me.

"... I know you don't want to, but she mentioned your guy Dredge ..."

That makes me sit up. Him. Again.

"... Apparently, she knows him. Look, I bet you'll be shaking your head, but just meet her will you, otherwise you'll make me look like a loser ..."

I'm not really listening to Gray's message now. He's gone to blah blah land.

"... Please, for me ... Think about it? I'll get her to text you. Arrange where to meet and that."

The message cuts off. I press '2' to repeat the message, as suggested by the disembodied woman with the sexy voice I'll never meet in a million years. Yes, he definitely says it.

Dredge.

I sit for a while, just thinking. I may be late for my rendezvous but I'm not sure, because I never wear a watch. Who wants to see their life ticking away in front of their eyes?

Eventually, I bang the car into gear. Miraculously, I'm not dead from either combustion or asphyxiation. I pull out the drive, neglecting to stop first and observe whether there's any traffic coming. But it's a cul-de-sac, so I'll probably be okay.

More's the pity.

I've my mysterious caller to meet and a shitload of questions bouncing around my empty head. Maybe I'll be able to reclaim the life that Gordon Dredge took away.

Tramp In Armour
There it was. Konstantin had been right.

Mr Lamb read the words for a second time. A small newspaper article on one of the inner pages, already twenty four hours out of date. Trivial. But not to Mr Lamb.

It said:

> **Corpse Found** Yesterday, a body was discovered by an elderly man walking his dog. Local sources named the deceased as James Hollowman, a partner at a prestigious London law firm. Police say they are investigating the cause of death, which is currently not being treated as suspicious.
> Reporter: David Brodie

Mr Lamb picked up his mobile phone, a cheap throwaway on a pay-as-you-go basis. No contracts, no paper or electronic trail to bring people almost as unscrupulous as him to his door.

He dialled the number from memory. Rang once before being answered. Like the recipient was waiting.

"Da?" Konstantin said.

Mr Lamb talked for ninety two seconds before he disconnected.

The second call was also to the UK, although the recipient was significantly more law-abiding than the Russian.

The third to a local travel agent.

Once completed, he pushed his chair back, walked out of the rented villa and onto the patio to absorb the vista.

The weather in Nice was comparatively cool this time of year, a touch of frost on the ground. The pool had long been covered over for the winter. Beneath him, the city dropped away until it met the Mediterranean, dotted with yachts, and just off shore crouched the airport.

Soon, he'd be on its tarmac, boarding a plane. A couple of hours flying and he'd be in his place of birth (Mr Lamb struggled to call anywhere home) and investigating whatever the hell was going on.

Until then, he had to wait.

His current client, a wealthy banker who had an apartment in Monaco, a few minutes' drive away, would be less than pleased that their contract was being terminated prematurely. He was not a man used to hearing bad news.

But that was just tough.

Mr Lamb, unmoved by the view, went back inside and started packing.

Superintendent Meadows sat at his expansive desk. Sighed. He was not a happy man. Despite everything, he was being drawn back there.

He'd hoped never to see this day. Never should have. The plans he had in progress he knew were sufficient, and the case was being handled proficiently. Another sigh. He should have known, though.

"If you want something doing well ..." and all that.

A couple of years ago, Meadows had arrested some high-profile bankers. His boss, the Chief of Police, had been implicated and, whilst evading a prison sentence, had been forced into retirement. A promotion and a shift to Organised Crime for Meadows had followed, then another into Fraud.

He owed all this to one man. The curiously named and infinitely well connected Mr Lamb. Who'd just called him and asked for the favour to be repaid.

Meadows skimmed the file, was very familiar with the subject, one Steven 'The Steroid' Oakhill, whose preferred method of execution for those who'd even mildly offended him was to throw them off a roof – height depending upon the scale of misdemeanour. To date Oakhill had successfully avoided every attempt to put him away. Had a smart lawyer defending him at every opportunity.

Meadows printed out most of the file, stuffed it into his bag. Entirely against regulations, but it had to be done. To get something, you had to give something.

Left his office to buy a day-return ticket to fucking Margate.

Angel's Wings

I've gone through my third set of lights without stopping (one green, two red). No impacts or even a near miss. Luck must be with me today, so perhaps I should consider investing in a lottery ticket. But I'll need to find a quid down the back of the seat first, 'cos there's a hole in my pocket. And my bank account.

I light a fag, which always helps me think.

My first call of the day. It had been distinctly odd. A very softly spoken, clearly well-bred man had asked me questions that I couldn't help but answer. Like:

Who are you?
Why are you interested in James Hollowman's death?
What do you know about the circumstances surrounding poor James' death?

Ordinarily, the sceptic (i.e. cynical as fuck) writer in me would have held everything close to my chest. A good reporter never gives anything away until the story is ready to print.

But that had been a different life, when I'd been good. Now I'm a self-employed hack desperate for any copy to earn a crust.

So what do I care if I spill all I know about some dead guy? It's not as I know much anyway.

I'd replied:

David Brodie, ace reporter. Who's asking?
I couldn't give half a dried shit. I just picked up the story from a contact on the force. Its business, you know?
He was found in a toilet, trousers round his ankles, head down in the bowl. Cause of death unclear at this stage, but sounds like he moved onto the next life having a good time in this one. Dirty boy.

For a moment there had been a stillness on the line. Made me think the call was imagined, but then the sibilant whisper came over the ether. Like he was trying not to be overheard.

"Do you think there had been foul play, Mr Brodie?" he'd asked.

Foul play? I thought. *Nobody says* that *anymore.*

Instead replied, "No idea, mate. I wasn't there."

"And what do you know of Gordon Dredge?"

I went totally, utterly silent. Stone dead. The world stopped spinning on its axis. Angels' wings no longer beat. Shit like that.

"Too fucking much. Why do you ask?"

"I remember your little, ah, problem with Gordon last year," he'd said, the tinkle of a titter in his tone.

An incredible understatement, that one. I'd spat, "So would a lot of people as I was front page news for weeks."

"What would you do if I said I could hand his head to you? On a platter."

My heart had caught in my throat. I didn't want to believe it, but I'd asked anyway, "With a bow on top?"

"As many as you would care to have."

Angels' wings had started beating again.

"I'd do anything."

"I rather hoped you would say that." I can still hear the stretched little smile in his voice.

And then he'd told me where to meet him.

Shark Bait

"Tosser!" Lucy shouted, giving some nutter in a battered car the finger. The driver had almost taken her out, had run the red light on the zebra crossing she was navigating.

"If I ever meet that guy, he's going to fucking regret it," Lucy muttered, and stomped on to her rendezvous with Gray.

A glass of wine awaited Lucy when she arrived. Gray handed it over, recognised the expression on her face. Had seen it too many times before, long in the past. Knew the cause. He'd hoped to never do so again. Couldn't help asking, though, "What happened?"

Got the full, fraught story.

"Look, I'm desperate, all right?" Lucy shot back, hurled some alcohol down her throat. Felt it hit her empty stomach, welcomed it like a lost friend.

"So desperate, you'd attempt to get into a fight with some random guy down an alley?" Gray was incredulous.

"We were on a bridge."

"Bridge, alley, whatever. Anything could have happened. Christ! What were you thinking?"

Lucy shrugged, whispered, "That's kind of the point, Gray. I miss it. The buzz. *Really* miss it."

"Raped. Or killed even." Gray visibly shuddered, hadn't heard Lucy's explanation, lost in his own world. She knew he saw darkness in every shadow – the prime reason he'd recently moved back home from London.

But so did Lucy. That ever-present fear of threat never quite got out from under your skin. An itch never quite scratched. Which was why she tried so hard to chase it down. To draw it back into her life, not run away from it.

"Hardly likely round here, is it?" Gloom shrouded her voice, because small seaside towns were not exactly the melting pots of extreme violence she craved.

"That's not the point, and you know it," he spat, sharp as a skewer. "All you need is one slice of bad luck, one 'wrong place, wrong time' moment." He stopped. Visibly shook himself. "Anyway, you've never listened to me. Why would you start now?"

She put a hand out, curled fingers around his forearm. "Gray …"

He smiled suddenly, shook her grip off. "Never mind! Let's get onto the real reason you're here."

Lucy sighed, defences up again. "Look, I've already told you. I'm not interested in a relationship."

Gray flapped his hands, trying to calm her down before the argument started over. "He's a decent bloke. Just fallen on hard times recently, what with his divorce."

"Great, so he's got a shitload of baggage. Join the club. Frankly, it's really not what I want right now."

"Well you need something, Luce. You can't carry on like you are."

"I've only one interest."

"Don't I know it!"

"And you know who can get me it."

"You worry me Lucy."

She shrugged.

Gray said, "What happens if I give you David and something goes wrong?"

"It's my life, Gray."

"I know, but I couldn't live with myself."

"Whatever." Lucy flicked his words away with a wave of her hand. She was seriously considering leaving. Couldn't stand the sanctimonious crap.

His mobile rang.

"Saved by the fucking bell," said Lucy, downing the rest of her drink.

He checked the screen, muttered, "I'd better take this. Sorry."

Gray stood up, moved away. Lucy shrugged her indifference to his rear.

"Hello, mate," she heard him say, despite the attempted low voice. "Unlike you to return a call."

She wiped at the large red lipstick mark on the rim of the glass. It smudged, looked like a splash of blood. She shuddered.

"Yes, I'm here with her now …"

Lucy pricked her ears up at that. She turned slightly, watched Gray out of the corner of her eye. He twisted his back on her, moved a few feet further away. Lucy stood, went to the bar, bought a double vodka.

Adjacent once more, she eavesdropped onto the one-sided conversation for the duration. Heard the name 'Dredge' several times. When it sounded like the dialogue was drawing to a conclusion, she quietly sat back down, leaving her drained glass behind. Tried hard to suppress the exultation. And fury.

"Sorry about that," Gray apologised again. He dropped his phone on the table. Pointed. "Want another?"

She nodded. Neglected to say that it would be her third. Whilst he was ordering, Lucy checked the caller ID. David Brodie. Memorised the number. Put the phone back down.

Gray returned to the table, just the one drink in hand. "Here you go," he said.

"That was David, asking what you know about Dredge. Whether you're for real."

Lucy raised an eyebrow. "Do I look real to you?"

Gray paled. Didn't like the look on her face. Failed to answer.

"What did you tell him?" she asked.

"Nothing, really, just said it was best coming from you."

"Good. Thank you."

Gray shook his head. Frustrated, worn down. Tugged a wallet out of his pocket and extracted a mangled piece of card. Handed it over like it was littered with highly contagious germs. "I hope I'm not going to regret this."

"Thank you." Lucy turned it over, looked at the name and number. One and the same.

Then she smiled, all tension gone. Another step on a long, long road.

"I'd better be going," Gray said. Looked like he was going to be ill.

"Okay. See you around," Lucy said as he left, barely masking the indifference in her voice. She pulled over his untouched lager. Poured it down her throat in one go. Bit of a celebration.

Gordon bastard Dredge.

Set an eel to catch a shark.

"You're fucking joking, right?" said Frank McGavin. His heavily tattooed arm extended out of the car window, shovel face wound into a grimace, tombstone teeth gritted.

"I ... wish ... I ... was ...," the attendant wheezed, primarily because Frank had him by the throat. The sovereign rings were digging into his flesh, windpipe seriously constricted.

Frank turned back to the three other equally tattooed men who were with him in the top of the range Merc. "Six quid! Did you hear that, lads?"

"Yeah, daylight robbery boss," said someone.

"Six fucking quid to drive a couple of miles," Frank said. Turned back to the attendant. "It's a bastarding liberty."

"Special discount?" the attendant croaked.

"How much?"

The suffocating man managed to look puzzled.

"Discount, you twat. How much?"

"Would six pounds be acceptable?"

"Entirely," Frank said equitably. Let the man go. Gave him a slight push so he was no longer bent over. The attendant staggered backwards. "Now, don't you go ringing the coppers, you hear me?"

"I wouldn't do that. I promise." The attendant rubbed his neck where there were thick red marks, each the size of a generous sausage.

"You look like a clever lad. But just as a bit of insurance ..." Frank nodded at one of the bruisers in the rear seat. "Squirrel, look after our boy here will you?"

"Ah, boss, do I have to?" he said.

"What do you fucking think?" Frank glared.

Squirrel gulped.

Without another word of protest, he popped the door, slid out of the back seat, slammed it shut behind him.

"Squirrel." He didn't hear. Frank hated repeating himself. "Squirrel!"

"Yeah, boss?"

"Fuck's sake. Ring me when he goes through," Frank said.

"Okay, boss."

"Don't get distracted."

"Okay, boss."

"See you shortly," Frank said and wound the window up.

As the car pulled away, Squirrel sighed. He always missed the fun. "So, what's there to do round here?"

The attendant eyed him nervously and rubbed at his throat some more. "Crossword?"

"Try again."

"TV?"

"Aye. That'll do."

Whitewash

Eighteen Months Ago

I've been investigating Gordon Dredge, scion of the investment world. He's like Alan Sugar's posh big brother. Loved by shareholders, hated by everyone else and about as successful. Wealthy, arrogant, loves to shout about how brilliant he is.

But there's a story. For years, rumours have persisted. Rumours that dirty money set him on the road to legitimate, fabulous wealth. Although it's never been proven. Another rumour – everyone who's ever investigated him has apparently been warned off. He's to be left alone.

I think it will be different for me.

Totally fucking wrong, could not be further from the truth. I am so up my own arse I can shake hands with my colon.

Naively, I get ready to take Dredge down. Am days away from doing so. Then I get a visit from the cops. Arrest warrant shoved in my face. They take my house apart. Cellar to loft. Floorboards up, ceilings down, the lot.

Scares the shit out of the kids. Missus is screaming, fit to rupture. The laptop gets bagged up and is carried outside for all to see by white suited and booted forensic men. Me, led out in handcuffs by cops sharply dressed for the occasion.

Flashbulbs burn. Turn night into day. Tomorrow, it's all over the papers.

They charge me with a raft of child sex offences. Apparently, photos are on my laptop. Claim they have witness statements going back years. It's a fucking lie, I promise you that. I've kids of my own. Never in a billion, trillion years would I ever do anything like that. If you're a parent, you'll understand.

The cops grill me for as long as they possibly can. Days it goes on for, all the while the stories being printed become more wild and lurid. Then the cops release me, throw me out into a baying mob of paparazzi and press. And that's that.

Accusations dropped. Unsubstantiated. I even get the laptop back. But shit sticks. Particularly the really shitty shit. Guilty, even if proven innocent.

First, I'm out of a job. 'Too infamous to be an investigative reporter' goes the claim. All the while, the missus keeps looking at me funny. Even though she says she believes me, I can tell she doesn't.

She hangs in for a couple of weeks, but eventually can't take the pressure anymore. Parents and so-called friends on at her constantly. So she boots me out, tells me I've been too focused on the job, not enough on the family. The wife keeps the London house, empties the holiday home. Annuls our marriage. For better or worse, eh?

It's then I lose it, just can't cope. I've nothing and no-one to anchor me. Entire days, weeks go missing. I've still little idea where I was or what I did. Most is a complete blank. I'd wake up battered, missing teeth, skinned knuckles. Then disappear into a bottle again.

One thing I clearly remember, though – contemplating suicide. Tried it too. Perhaps my most lucid action of the period. But, throughout, I cling on to one thing. Not the wife, or the kids. No.

My sharpest recollection from that whole episode. A copper I'd not seen before entered my cell. Well dressed, clearly senior. Angular face, downturned mouth. In garlic soft tones told me it was all my fault, that I should have left Gordon Dredge alone and to do so in the future. The businessman had real friends. I didn't.

So, you see, I owe him, Gordon Dredge.

BIG time.

Homeward Bound

Five Days Ago

"Any baggage to check in, sir?" the Air France attendant enquired.

Mr Lamb shook his head. "Carry-on only."

He watched the woman eye his diplomatic tag with disinterest. There was always somebody ostentatious travelling through Nice airport. It was par for the course. Government officials were ten a penny and he knew he looked entirely innocuous, which was the desired effect.

She stifled a yawn. Handed him passport, ticket and fast track pass. "Have a good flight, sir."

Forty five minutes later and Mr Lamb was aboard the plane, strapped in, keen to take off. He'd decided to fly business class, to pay the extra despite the ridiculously short transit time. Just felt like spending some of his ill-gotten gains on frivolous fringe benefits for once.

He heard a beep, felt a little jarring in his pocket. A text.

Although the stewardesses were sweeping the cabin to ensure passengers were belted up, he checked the message. The blonde glanced down into his lap as she passed, turned a blind eye to the phone. One of the privileges of business class. In economy, he'd have been summarily executed for daring to have an electronic device still engaged.

It was from Konstantin. A very brief summary of Gordon Dredge and his apparently questionable business activities. He didn't sound like a particularly philanthropic individual, but then the wealthy and powerful rarely were in his experience. Mr Lamb powered down his phone and slid it into his jacket pocket.

Someone said, "Good trip?"

Mr Lamb glanced over at the man sitting next to him. Sober suit, dull tie, glasses. Banker for sure. He'd had enough of this breed – so had most of the world.

"No." Glared at the man, watched him take in his lean face, severe expressionless features, coal black eyes. Saw the failure to suppress a shudder.

"Okay. Good to hear," the banker tripped over his words. Opened his Financial Times to its full extent, hid behind it.

Mr Lamb mentally chided his childish behaviour. Konstantin's influence, he knew.

But then overhead speakers crackled. A voice drifted out, "Cabin crew, ready for take-off."

They obeyed and a minute later engines flared. Propelled the plane along the runway which wobbled into the air.

Superintendent Meadows stared absently out of the window at the countryside rattling past. Houses, trees, bland crap.

He was thinking hard.

Fucking Margate.

Four!

Unfortunately, we hadn't arranged to meet at the sort of cheap, down-at-heel dump that's more me. Oh no. Only some relatively exclusive golf clubhouse, right on the coast. There's even a charge to use the private road.

Six quid!

Thank Christ they waive it for club members and guests, because I'd have had to sell my body to raise that sort of cash and, trust me, no-one wants to see that. Put you right off your breakfast.

Thankfully, the guy who peeps out of the ticket booth window as I approach clearly sees my car is worth less than the fee, so he waves me through without stepping into the cold and I don't have to deliver my less than well-honed sob story. What a lazy bastard, though.

There are speed bumps on the road that leads me through the indolent housing estate. I graze the exhaust over every one – a few more scrapes to add to the gapes. Looking at the size of the edifices, they really don't need the extra cash the levy generates. Another example of applying power because you can.

Soon a sharp left, and another half mile or so of jolts which makes me feel like I'm on the sea, rather than running directly parallel to it. At last, when I'm considering throwing up, the new build facility heaves into view.

I exit the Shit Machine, look over the Merc I've parked next to. It's shiny, brand new, top of the range. The engine ticks idly as it cools. Nice, but too flash. I prefer mine.

I slam the door a couple of times, don't bother locking up, enter the clubhouse reception. It's small, well decorated, couple of plants, some golfing pictures on the wall and a desk with a lad sat behind it.

"Hi," I say. Because my mother brought me up to be polite. "I'm looking for a Mr Gowan."

The receptionist, spotty oik with Harry Potter glasses, looks puzzled. "Not familiar with that name."

"He's a member, I believe."

"No. He's not."

"Do you know everyone here?" Already my vocal fangs are out, sarcasm drips from them onto the floor. Better be careful, I might slip in it.

"Pretty much, yes," Oik says. Looks at me, like it's game over.

"Would you mind checking?"

Huffs like a British Airways air hostess, but turns round, says over his shoulder into the office behind, "Phyllis, know a Gowan?"

A hefty woman emerges. She barely fits through the doorway. Expansive is an understatement, but the smile I deliver her is on an even grander scale.

"No Gowan here, love. I know all the members. Sorry."

"What about guests?"

"No," states Oik, reclaiming centre stage.

"That's a remarkably good memory you possess there."

Oik pushes a pad towards me with a single digit. The one on which guests sign in. He's correct, there's no Gowan listed.

"Ah."

Thankfully, I've been in way too many other situations where embarrassment results from my own inconsiderate / unintelligent / tactless behaviour. This is a basic little misdemeanour in comparison. "Well, if you do have someone arrive by that name can you give me a call?"

Oik looks at me. "What number?" he says.

"You've lost me, mate."

"What telephone number do you expect us to call you on? Do I look like Derren Brown?"

Nothing further could be further from reality. I happen to like the maestro of deception. Not Oik, he's a git.

However, I have to admit he's onto something. To resolve the situation, I dig around in a pocket. Extract several pieces of fluff, a stick of chewing gum (minus wrapper), some coins and, finally, a bent business card I'd had printed in a railway station machine ages ago.

"Got a pen?" I ask.

Single finger pushes one at me.

I cross the mobile number out, replace it with my latest one, then hand over the battered bit of card with pride. Oik takes it and, keeping his eyes on me, deposits it in the bin. He bares his teeth at me in a fake smile. I have that effect on people.

"So you won't be calling me, then."

Shake of the head. "Against club rules."

I wish he'd told me that previously. But I say, "In that case can I have the card back? It's my only one."

He retrieves the worn rectangle, now a little more stained. Tosses it over the counter.

"Goodbye, sir," Oik says.

Phyllis looks at him with something approaching admiration. It might be the start of a beautiful relationship and it's all down to me.

"Yeah, cheers for that," I say and sweep my meagre possessions into the palm of my hand. I retreat with absolutely no dignity intact. On the other hand, I didn't enter with any, if truth be told. On a positive note, at least I've a stick of gum which I start chewing, fluff and all.

Back outside, it's bloody windy. The coastline is entirely exposed. To the fore is a wide swath of brown, choppy sea that looks entirely uninviting. A sliver of yellow-ish sand separates me from the water. To the left is Thanet itself and to the right, the land stretching away into nothingness. Bleak.

Behind lies the golf course. No-one in their right mind should be playing today, but, incredibly, there are a few lunatics out lugging heavy bags of metal sticks. They're trudging into the distance and, in moments, disappear. It seems to be one of those sports that its participants can't get enough of and vice versa. Personally, I don't understand it.

But maybe that's why I've no mates, because they're all playing fucking golf. I stand impotently, not sure what to do next.

I admit it to myself then. Despite my claims to Gray's voicemail, I have nothing on. My petrol tank is as empty as my wallet. I haven't a number on which to call Gowan – when I scroll down, the registry reads 'Unknown.' I'm totally stuck. Then the phone rings in my hand.

Three times in a day. Wonders never cease.

A Rather Blunt Missive

The driver furrowed his brow. Applied the brakes, brought the articulated truck to a stop. Said, "What the hell?"

The source of his puzzlement was a man. Standing in the middle of the road, hands by his sides. The driver looked at his companion, who took a firmer grip on his gun. The driver blew his horn. Idiot in the road wouldn't budge, did the thousand yard stare thing.

"I'll sort this out," the guard grunted. Opened his door, slid out.

The driver craned his neck, looking downwards. Thought he'd enjoy the spectacle of brief violence. But his protector didn't appear.

Before he could think, the driver's door was pulled open. He yelped as he was dragged out of the cab. He hit the ground heavily, started to protest until he saw the guard knelt on the tarmac, his own firearm pressed against his temple by a stone-faced killer.

The driver sensed a man crouch down next to him. Had to turn his head to see who. Took in browned skin, short dark hair shot through with grey, hard eyes and a scar that ran across his cheek and puckered his chin.

"My apologies for your treatment," the scarred man said.

"That's okay," the driver stammered. Didn't mean it, but wanted to avoid upsetting the guy.

"May I ask, what is your name?" Perfect English, but creased with an accent the driver didn't recognise.

"Paul. Please, I've got a wife and kids." Another lie, but needs must.

"It is all right, Paul. No harm will come to you personally. But I'm afraid I will be taking your lorry."

"Yeah, have it. It ain't mine anyway."

"It wasn't a request, but thank you anyway," the scarred man said with a small grin.

The driver nervously smiled back.

"And, Paul, I'd like you to take two messages back to your boss, Mr Oakhill. Would you do that for me?"

"Sure!"

"Good. Please inform him that Adam will be in touch shortly to negotiate the transfer of his business over to me. Can you remember that?"

Paul nodded. "Yeah, but I don't understand."

"You don't need to. Just tell him what I said."

"Okay."

Paul didn't want to ask, but had to. "You said there were two messages."

"You are correct, I did. I can see you are a smart guy."

Paul jerked with the sudden gunshot, stared as his companion toppled over, half his head missing, the rest splattered across the road.

As he threw up, heard, "Goodbye Paul."

Was still retching when the truck pulled away. He briefly glimpsed Adam waving nonchalantly, like he was heading off on a summer holiday.

Dead Man's Tale

So my phone's ringing and someone on the peak of a sand dune is waving. Maybe it's a golfer signalling to his mates. Ball's in the sand or some other bollocks.

The figure waves again with a little more urgency. I look around. There's me, the building, some cars and a few flappy little flags to show where the little holes are located for the little balls to drop down into.

But no-one and nothing else. My phone stops ringing. The figure holds a hand up, something in it. Lowers it. Ringing again.

"Hello?"

"Mr Brodie, Mr Gowan here."

"Oh good. Look, I'm at the clubhouse, but you're not."

"That is correct. It's me waving at you. From the beach."

"Ah."

"Would you care to join me?"

"Sure."

I feel like a right dick now.

Get walking, pass a bin, eject the gum from my jaws, the fluff is proving a bit too much of a challenge. Feet sink into the sand. It hisses as it shifts. The bank rises in front of me which, once I make the peak, drops away again into an incline towards the sea, shallow but enough to mask most of the building at its base.

I stop, look around. There's a person seated, back to me, looking out to sea. I stand over him.

"Beautiful here, isn't it?" he says. "Wide open space. Peaceful."

"I guess so." Give me a town any day. "Mr Gowan I presume?"

Turns to me, looks up, all formal and knobby like. Says, "Well of course, who else?" Disdain clear in his clipped, public schoolboy tone.

"Have to be careful in my game." It's a crap defence and we both know it.

"Take a pew," he says and pats the sand next to him. It looks a bit wet. My arse discovers that the deduction derived by my eyes is totally correct.

"Sorry to be so ... melodramatic with the setting," says Gowan. I twist a little to see him better. A small man, moustache lodged above a narrow mouth unused to displaying amusement, greying hair, glasses. Entirely unremarkable. "But, unfortunately, it's quite necessary because, you see, I'm dead."

I laugh for a few moments. He doesn't join in. My cackle dies away on the breeze.

"I can see you'd benefit from an explanation," he says.

"Mind if I smoke? 'Cos if you're dead, I assume you're not bothered about something as mundane as cancer."

He gives me a thin smile with those thin lips.

"It's difficult to find amusement in anything when once one had everything and now one has nothing."

"Very deep." I take a draw on my fag, ignore the fact I understand his perspective entirely. "What do you want, because my backside is getting wet."

"I've been asking people about you."

"People?"

He goes on as if he hasn't heard me. "Long story short, you're a man that's severely down on his luck and in need of a break before you end up in the gutter, never to reappear."

Mind reader. Doesn't look like Derren though. If he was, I'd ask him for his autograph. Then sell it on eBay. Retire.

"Look, if you're just here to insult me, I'll take my increasingly damp backside back to my car," I say. I can hear the petulance in my voice, but I don't care. I hate posh people speaking to me like that. Well, actually, like anything.

"I was being literal. I want to help you."

"How?"

"By telling you all about Gordon Dredge. Would that be of benefit to you, perhaps, David?"

I sigh. No choice really. He's got me. Had before I'd even arrived.

"Five minutes, that's all I've got."

It takes a lot longer than that. Eventually, I get up and leave Gowan on the beach.

And that's when everything goes to shit.

Death In Sandwich

Wheels kissed concrete. Jets roared as the pilot threw the engines into reverse, arresting the plane's forward motion. The sudden reapplication of friction rocked the passengers in unison from side to side.

Mr Lamb floated up out of his meditative state as the welcoming platitudes of the pilot washed over him. To the casual observer, he'd have appeared asleep, but his voluntarily induced vegetation was far more refreshing.

He unbuckled as the plane drew up to the stand. Immediately the seatbelt sign dropped, he stood, opened the overhead locker, pulled out his small case. The banker remained firmly in place, tucked behind his newspaper. Mr Lamb ignored him, moved to the front of the plane and exuded serenity whilst he waited to exit.

The blonde stewardess peered through a tiny window situated in the door, waved at the ground staff and manipulated the monstrous lever. It popped open and slid away.

"Goodbye, sir. Have a good day," said the stewardess and flashed a smile.

Mr Lamb stepped onto English soil for the first time in several years.

He hoped she would be proven right.

Frank McGavin didn't enjoy the feeling of sand under his feet. It shifted too easily, made his footing insecure. For a man who demanded certainty, it was simply unnerving. Not that he'd ever admit that to anyone. Thankfully, he reached the top of a dune, settled down to watch and wait. As Gowan had already killed himself, Frank's only task was to ensure the dead man finally did the deed.

The other two were in the car. Fuck knows what they'd do with themselves, but he didn't care. So long as they stayed out of the way. This was his job alone.

Quickly, got bored.

His attention drifted to the twats playing golf. Couldn't think of a stupider game. Snooker or darts. That's what he preferred. Inside, with a beer and a fag, with limited opportunity to be out of breath. No chance of getting cold and wet.

He was feeling pretty frosted by the time the pair's summit concluded. A couple of nips of malt whisky from his hip flask had provided limited relief. A smoke would have been better, but he hadn't wanted to alert them.

Conveniently, Gowan remained looking out to sea, as if he'd never seen the wet stuff before, whilst Brodie pissed off. Frank could hear the rattle and scrape of the exhaust as the reporter drove past. He let the sound fade, stood, adjusted his leather jacket back to nonchalant proportions and picked his way over the unstable ground.

Frank saw a flicker of something in Gowan's eyes when he appeared at his side. Fear? No, more like resignation.

"How did I do?" Gowan asked tentatively.

"Not bad for a geek."

Gowan seemed relieved, said, "He'd be very upset if he knew you'd given the reporter everything."

Frank laughed. Upset. Now there was an understatement.

Gowan asked, "What's next?"

Frank didn't answer for a moment, let the moment expand, then said, "Of course, I can't let you go."

Gowan shrugged, like it was of no consequence. "You'd have killed me eventually."

"Probably. Any last requests? Fag or something?"

Gowan didn't answer, just stared out at the waves, as though made of stone. Frank idly wondered how it felt when you knew, *really knew*, this was your last moment on earth. Then he mentally shrugged. It'd be a long time before it was his turn to experience his own mortality and, if he had his way, at the end he'd be on top of a hot woman.

Frank smiled at the thought, then grabbed Gowan and dragged him into the freezing cold waves until the water was knee deep.

The little man barely resisted. It felt to Frank like he was taking a reluctant terrier along for a walk. However, it took longer than he'd expected for Gowan to succumb. There was some thrashing and kicking as the natural survival instinct kicked in, but nothing Frank hadn't experienced before.

Once Gowan stopped struggling, Frank held him under for another half a minute, just to be sure. He let the corpse float to the surface. Gave it a little push so the current took it. Maybe it would wash Gowan well out to sea. Maybe it wouldn't. You never knew around here and he didn't care.

Frank pulled one foot, then the other, out of the sucking sand and made his way back to the Mercedes. The killing had made the blood sing in his veins. His heart rate was elevated, so he didn't mind one little bit that he was half soaked through.

But Frank's good mood soured when he discovered his two idiots pissing about on the golf course with some sulky member's gear. He surveyed the wreckage. Most of the guy's clubs were bent and at least one ball had gone through the clubhouse window.

"Come on," Frank barked. "Time to go."

"But we're having fun!" Tyrone replied, sounding like a child. He caught Frank's expression, dropped the club on the green, and shifted.

Mr Lamb, thanks to his diplomatic authorisation, circumvented the queue at passport control, and was soon exiting the terminal building. It was much colder than France. A stinging sleet pummelled the air, breath frosted.

His phone signalled the receipt of a text. The message told him in which bay the car he'd asked for was parked. He found it, bent down quickly, retrieved the magnetic box from behind the bumper. Inside was the ignition key.

He started up the Honda. After a variety of laborious health and safety warnings, the sat-nav kicked in. Mr Lamb entered Konstantin's address from memory and, whilst the device hunted for a signal, pulled out of the car park. A ticket was tucked in the visor, which he slid into the machine and the barrier rose. Within five minutes, he was onto the M11 and heading south.

He didn't drive quickly, didn't drive slowly, was assertive but not aggressive. In other words, he drove in a fashion which meant he got from A to B as quickly as you can in the UK without attracting the attention of the authorities. Close examination he could do without.

It was simply a waste of precious time.

The Merc pulled up at the deserted gatehouse.

Frank said, "Where is that useless fucker? Bang the horn, Tyrone."

Squirrel poked his head out at the insistent beeps. Frank waved at him and a moment later, he was squeezing into the car. The attendant hovered at the doorway.

Frank wound the window down, crooked a finger. The attendant walked over, but stayed out of reach. Frank grinned.

"I can see that you're a clever boy. You've learnt from your experience. Well done. So here's the next lesson. I know where you live. With a little effort, I could find out where your entire family live. If I hear a word spoken about today, I'll visit everyone you're close to then, last of all, I'll come knocking at your door. I promise it won't be an enjoyable experience, or a survivable one either. So, do yourself a favour, and keep it shut. Okay?"

The attendant nodded his head. He looked like he was going to piss himself. Frank knew whether people accepted a warning or not. It was in the eyes. This guy well and truly had. He wouldn't be any bother.

"Let's go," Frank said as the window wound up.

Only when the Merc was out of sight did the attendant release his bladder. He decided he was going to get a new job a long, long way from here.

The Gloom

It's the late afternoon and I'm back in my house, specifically in my living room. Total contents:

Me.
A knackered armchair (which I'm inhabiting).
My crap mobile phone.
Three cans of whatever beer was on special offer (note that these are purely temporary residents).
A smouldering fag (no ash tray, just the floor).

For illumination, a single light bulb burns weakly above my head. No shade, just a few cobwebs stretching from cable to ceiling that cast interesting skeins on the wall where pictures once hung.

Somewhere in the corner my depression skulks, ignoring me after I throw a couple of tinnies, drained of their contents, of course, in its direction.

The room is a reflection of the rest of the property. As I've said before, the missus took the lot. There's barely a stick of furniture left. My current arse receptacle is a reclaim from a skip.

It feels huge now, like when we first moved in. Loads of space, most of it superfluous. Then proceeded to fill in the gaps with stuff, a process which accelerated once the kids arrived. Then the complaints began about how little room there really was.

The missus wanted to buy a larger place, but I refused. It was a weekend home, after all. She bought new crap to replace the old crap, but couldn't bear to be parted with the old crap, so it got put in the loft. Guess what? The missus suddenly wanted it when she departed.

Bugger spring cleaning, just dissolve your marriage, relationship, whatever, and let the lesser half cart the clutter away for you.

Anyway ... I'm sat in my chair, mobile phone in one hand, beer in the other, fag between my lips. I've learnt over the years that I have a shit memory. For example, I typically neglect to recall where I've left something, or I'm unable to put a name to a face, or remember where I'm supposed to be at any one given time. Which, for a reporter, isn't ideal. So I'd recorded the whole conversation with Gowan on my mobile.

Along with the sound of some waves, an irate seagull and a livid golfer.

Harbour Lights

Konstantin was already seated at a small table when Mr Lamb entered the café, a windswept building at the end of the harbour arm, once a coastguard facility turned to new uses. He'd driven straight here from the airport and was slightly tired.

The Russian had his back to the wall, positioned so he could take in the entire interior at a glance. Mr Lamb scanned the room, saw no danger, let the door close behind him and walked over.

He pulled out a chair adjacent to Konstantin. Rested his arms on the table, hands in full view. Old habits die hard. Even though they weren't enemies anymore.

"Americano, extra shot, hot milk," Mr Lamb said to Julie, according to the name badge, who appeared to take his order. She tucked a strand of hair behind an ear. Poked her tongue out of the corner of her mouth whilst concentrating on writing down the order. Konstantin shook his head at Julie's questioning look, happy with his strawberry milkshake.

"Would you care for anything to eat?" she asked. "Mackerel's on special today. Fresh off the boat." Julie nodded out the window, towards the smacks tied up against the wharf.

"Nŏ, thank you."

She bustled away, unaffected by Mr Lamb's rejection of the café's culinary delights.

Light and airy, the views from within were spectacular – onto the harbour one side, full of pleasure boats and working craft, and the North Sea on the other. A passenger ferry was in the process of nosing its way into the shipping lane, heading to Belgium. The establishment was less than a quarter full. Families and fishermen. No dubious characters – besides Konstantin and himself.

The Russian looked totally different to yesterday, unrecognisably so. Which was the point, really. The critical alteration was he'd showered. His grey hair was tied back into a ponytail and the previously unkempt beard, where a family of rats would have thought twice about inhabiting, was groomed and braided. The greenish coat had been discarded, and instead he wore leather trousers, a t-shirt and a leather waistcoat. There was even a motorbike outside, a Royal Enfield Bullet, and a helmet on the table to complete the image.

"Good flight?" Konstantin asked. He sucked noisily on the straws. Mr Lamb saw the twinkle in the reformed tramp's eye, refused to be drawn.

"Anything's acceptable in comparison to an army transport plane."

"Very true." Konstantin smiled ruefully. "When he arriving?"

"Any time now."

The pair fell silent as the waitress delivered the coffee. Mr Lamb poured the milk into the cup. Warm to the touch, which was good. He watched the colour of the liquid lighten as the pairing swirled and combined.

"While we wait, what do we know about James?"

Konstantin pushed his half-finished milkshake to one side. "Last job was partner at London firm of accountants. Before that, briefly with Dredge Industries: CEO and Chairman, one Gordon Dredge."

The Russian handed over a manila file. Mr Lamb ignored the in-joke and opened it, tipped towards him so nobody else could observe the contents. He examined the photograph. A strong face, one used to decisions that went his way. Full head of grey hair, arrogant sneer to the mouth. Running to fat. Wealthy, but not necessarily happy and healthy.

"What's their business?"

"Was."

"Went bust?"

Konstantin nodded. "Da. But when operational, blah-blah, very technical, but essentially biochemistry, wonder drug. Investors slathered over Dredge, threw cash at him. Very wealthy man on company valuation alone."

"James was on the money side, wasn't he?"

"Finance Director. Thirteen weeks. Left suddenly."

"Long enough to know how the place ticked." Mr Lamb drank some coffee. It was better than he'd expected. "What's this Dredge like?"

"As person, not popular with staff. In business, maverick. Started and sold three companies. Very rich, very quickly. All gone now."

"Bad deals?"

"No-one saying. Hard to tell, tough times for business in last few years. Lots gone to wall that may have survived in better years."

The door went again. Konstantin and Mr Lamb looked up at the entrant. Tall, sober suit, angular face, down-turned mouth.

"That him?" Konstantin asked, scrutinising the man who had 'cop' written all over his attitude.

"Yes," Mr Lamb said, and slid the file out of sight.

Meadows must have felt Konstantin's gaze because he slid his eyes onto their table. A flash of acknowledgment as he registered Mr Lamb, a query with Konstantin. He came and sat down. The table suddenly seemed crowded.

"Gentlemen," Meadows said. "You'll excuse me if I don't show you my ID." He smiled. No response. Held his hand out to shake. No movement from either.

"You must have me confused with someone else," Konstantin said. Mr Lamb heard razors in his voice. The Russian inflection was gone too. "I would never pretend to be such."

The waitress appeared. Meadows waved her away, said, "I'm not staying long." When she was gone, he said, "For some reason we seem to have got off to a bad start."

"No," Konstantin replied. "I just don't like you."

"I'm not here to take abuse."

"Then you're welcome to leave."

"Can we get down to business?" Mr Lamb cut in. He was used to his Russian friend taking instant, and usually negative, positions on people he met, based only on instinct. "We're here for one thing, which is to find James' killer. Can you two put whatever it is away for now?"

"Yes," Konstantin said, after an eye from Mr Lamb.

Meadows nodded. Didn't look like he really agreed.

"Specifically, I'm not interested in Hollowman," Meadows said. "That's a job for my colleagues. However, Gordon Dredge and his association with Steven Oakhill is another matter."

"Why?"

"Dredge is under investigation by the Financial Services Authority over problems with his business – alleged fraud and insider dealing for a start, but that's relatively minor. Oakhill is the big fish I want to land. So I'll help you get justice for Hollowman, if you help me put Oakhill down."

"Precisely who is Oakhill?" Mr Lamb asked.

"Local gang leader, the top of the pile around here. I'm not surprised you've never heard of him. Keeps himself to himself. Lives out in the marshes, gets all of his strong arm stuff done by one Frank McGavin."

"Keep going."

Meadows spoke in a monotone, like he was reading directly from a record, "Steven Arthur Oakhill, AKA Stevie The Steroid. Small-time criminal in his youth, nothing serious. Got into boxing, was a bit of a wimp. Started taking anabolic steroids to beef himself up, hence the nickname. Got banned after losing it in the ring and nearly killing some kid. Then his illegal activities stepped up. Became formally associated with a school friend, Frank McGavin. Formed a criminal gang, which started small, but now they're into everything – prostitution, extortion, people smuggling, drugs, murder."

"Sounds like my kind of guy," Konstantin said.

Meadows leaned over, looked straight into the Russian's eyes. Neither blinked. Meadows said, "He's fucking mental. He's either as happy as Larry's extra-enthusiastic brother, or as down and depressed as a vegan at a hog roast. He can flip from one to the other in moments. He's a risk-taker, particularly with other people's lives. He'll do pretty much anything. There's no knowing what he'd get up to from one moment to the next."

"Sounds like you know him very well," Mr Lamb said.

Meadows shrugged. "It happens when you've been on a case for a while, seen the damage one man can cause." He held out an A4 envelope. "I'm breaking several regulations just giving you this."

Mr Lamb took the envelope. He asked, "You've an insider? Someone in the gang?"

"You know I can't confirm or deny that. Here's my number, should you wish to reach me." The cop handed over a business card.

"Where will you be staying?"

He laughed sharply. "Not around here, that's for sure. Straight back to London for me." Meadows stood up, didn't bother holding out a hand to shake this time. He'd learnt. "I'll be in touch soon."

"I not trust him," Konstantin said as soon as the door shut on Meadows' back. The accent had returned.

"You made that pretty obvious."

"There something about him. Not put my finger on it."

"That's largely irrelevant. We need him at the moment."

Mr Lamb pulled a handful of pages from the envelope. Dredge's finances. It would need time to digest, but there was a brief summary document pinned to the front. It surmised the man was in trouble.

A few years ago, his assets were strong, but no longer. He'd recently liquidated all his stocks, but had virtually no cash and the house was mortgaged several times over. Not that the banks who'd provided the loans knew about the others.

"He's bankrupt."

"Good." Konstantin slurped on his milkshake, wiped his beard. "What next?"

"Work the details," Mr Lamb said. "The answer is always in the minutiae."

Konstantin grimaced. In his experience a gun usually generated instant answers, if not messier results.

The camera whirred as it captured image after image as they left the café. Distance shots and close-ups in high definition colour recorded the features of Meadows, then Konstantin and Mr Lamb in fine detail.

The photographer looked at the pictures. "Know either of them?" he asked.

"One," a man called Troon said. "And he's fucking bad news."

Troon pulled out his mobile, made a call, said, "It's me. It went down as you thought. But we've a problem …" Troon paused as Konstantin roared by on his Bullet, the exhaust loud, throaty. "Lamb is in on the act."

"Fuck."

Waited whilst his boss thought. Eventually, he said, "You'll have to make contact."

Troon's heart sank.

Grave Consequences

The dictation continues.

"Go on." That's me.

"Gordon Dredge, biggest bastard that walked the earth." Brian Gowan sounds cultured, well-educated and wealthy, even over the tinny tiny speaker. And like he's swearing for the first time in his life. "I work for him, used to work for him I should say. I was his Chief Operating Officer, Dredge's number two in our little business venture. He was the figurehead, I was the one that made it all happen. Whilst Gordon was hobnobbing with other *powerhouses of industry*." Gowan had made sarcastic speech marks with his fingers at that.

"I was working, ensuring the business ran smoothly. The staff got paid, materials were bought. We delayed remunerating suppliers, forced customers to pay us as fast as possible, that kind of thing. Day-to-day activity. I was the oil that smoothed the meshing cogs."

"Cogs, right. Understood."

There's a brief silence, filled with whistling of wind.

"I see I'm still not getting through."

"No, no, I'm really interested, honest." Actually, at this point, I was looking over my shoulder at an angry golfer.

"The oil I all-too-subtly referred to was the movement of money that made transactions happen. No commerce otherwise."

Two guys had just joined the golfer, taken his clubs and started whacking balls around.

"Okay," I say, more absorbed by what's happening on the green. "What was the business?"

"We made a fantastic product, really high-tech material. I won't bore you with the details. Unless you've a PhD in biochemistry, it won't mean a thing to you anyway. But it was a drug of the future, today. And Gordon brought in money to exploit the opportunity. Lots of it. That's his strength, he's very convincing. He can sell anything to anyone. Particularly dreams to the gullible. Millions poured forth."

"Millions? Of pounds?" I'm interested again.

"Yes, from pension funds, private investments, banks, the lot. Everyone was in on it. The staff had share option schemes, contributory of course. Greedy shareholders expected a huge return against a supposed almost-zero risk. But it was all a sham. There's always a potential downside, but ours was huge. The product simply didn't work. Early tests were fine, however approvals weren't gained. The clinical data spoke for itself.

"We had to announce the problems. Investors took fright. The investors wanted their money back, but we just didn't have it. We couldn't pay staff or our suppliers either. No-one wanted to give us any more working capital. Ultimately, Gordon pulled the plug. Lots of people lost their jobs."

"You'd over oiled the cogs, then?"

"No, no. I'm sure of one thing," Gowan says, sidestepping the irony. "Although some of the cash had gone on normal operating expenses, the majority of it should have still been there. The balance sheet had been strong, whatever Gordon said. The whole Board knew it."

Silence again. Gowan had looked at a squawking seagull. Maybe recalling better times.

I remembered I'd an increasingly damp backside. "Go on," I say.

Dragged out sigh from Gowan.

"Before the company went bust, I went to see him one morning. I told him we should come clean, reveal our position to the investors. Gordon went ballistic, said that if we did that I'd be ruined. *Me*, not him. It didn't really sink in at first. But he made sure it did. He told me that as COO, it was all *my* responsibility. He hadn't *really* been in control of the business, he was simply a facilitator. Rubbish like that. Said I was finished, that my family would be just a memory, I'd never work again, I'd go to prison for fraud. Unless ..."

"What?"

"I killed myself."

"Did you?" I cringe as I hear a repeat of perhaps the dumbest question I've ever posed since 'Will you marry me?'

"No. And yes."

"Sorry, you'll need to run that by me again."

"I left Gordon in his office. He had this huge smile on his face. If he'd have confessed right there and then to being the devil incarnate, I'd have believed him. I got in my car, drove to God knows where, but it was by water. I left a suicide note in my car, said sorry to my wife, prayed and threw myself in."

"What, and you washed up somewhere after surviving for hours in freezing conditions? You'd lost your memory until today?"

"No. The water was only six inches deep. Soaked me to the skin, shocked me out of my stupor. I lay in the stream for a while, just thinking. I decided to do it all over again, but better prepared."

"Hurled yourself into a puddle for a second time?"

"No flight involved at all. Just the façade of the process. I spent the next 24 hours setting my affairs in order, then returned. Like that idiot in the North East who pretended to drown in a kayaking accident a couple of years ago. I left behind plenty of clues, but no body and no suicide note. And I won't be stupid enough to walk into a police station and confess."

"But something went wrong."

Gowan turns and looks at me.

"Perhaps you're not as unintelligent as you appear at first glance."

"Thanks." I don't mean it, by the way.

"Hardly has my corpse metaphorically begun to cool than Gordon is onto the investors. He told them that *I* had the money *and* the chemical formula to the drug on a USB stick and both had disappeared with me."

"So then it's really just you to blame."

There's silence on the tape, but he'd nodded whilst his eyes blazed with barely suppressed anger.

"I remember something about it in the press, but I wasn't in a good place then," I say. Pissed up actually, and lamenting the beginnings of my separation in the depths of a vodka bottle.

"Yes. It was everywhere. A major scandal. And Gordon came out the other side. Slightly tainted, but free to carry on. Plus a hell of a lot wealthier, I expect."

"And you were incommunicado?"

"Yes, until I saw your newspaper article about poor James."

"Uh-huh."

Thinking, *So?*

"You see, James Hollowman was our Finance Director. If anyone else knew what was going on, where the money was, it would be him. And now he's dead too. You said there were no suspicious circumstances, but I don't believe it. It's all too convenient. And he's not the first employee to die."

That made me prick my ears up.

"And where to I come in to all this?"

"You're a reporter and I want to give you the story ..."

Dead Zone

Mr Lamb excelled at both breaking (bones) and entering (classified spaces). However, tonight he tended towards the latter.

He and Konstantin had gained admission to the morgue with ridiculous ease. This he'd anticipated, because the authorities wouldn't expect anyone who was alive to want to access the miserable place and certainly no-one already inside would prove capable of escaping.

Mr Lamb, however, wasn't at all bothered by his surroundings. He didn't believe in ghosts, the after-life, or any of that nonsense. He'd seen the light go out in far too many people to consider any option other than there being nothing but darkness after death.

He briefly shone a pencil-light around to get his bearings. He could feel Konstantin at his side. The beam was narrow, but extremely powerful. It illuminated a small reception area, tables, chairs, vending machine. Mr Lamb flicked the torch off almost immediately, didn't want to take the slightest chance that someone may see existence where there was only supposed to be the expired.

On a more practical level, he wanted to preserve his night vision. Neither he nor Konstantin wore low-light goggles. If they were caught, it would be hard enough explaining their presence. Doubly so with military equipment.

In a matter of moments, the pair was through the waiting area and into a corridor. Closed doors were peppered along its length. He pointed at the offices and left Konstantin to access whatever electronic data he could find.

Mr Lamb continued to where the bodies were stored – the cold room at the passage's termination. He entered. It was a wide open space with accommodation facilities for the corpses set into the wall. The temperature was noticeably lower within. Mr Lamb scanned down the chart until he found the name he wanted and crossed to the corresponding drawer. It moved easily on well-oiled runners, despite the weight. Even chillier air seeped out.

Inside lay a body-shaped shroud. He pulled the cloth back from the face. It was hard to see the features in the dim light, so Mr Lamb shone the beam down, illuminating a familiar face.

James Hollowman.

But Mr Lamb couldn't consider this lump of flesh decaying at an arrested rate to be anything other than an 'it'. The expression was one of peace, features relaxed, skin as pale and brittle as parchment. There was no humanity within. Whatever a soul was, it had left long ago. Now just a wisp, scattered particles.

He peeled the cloth down the chest and to James' hips, the beam following a clear incision that ran the length of the torso that had been roughly closed up. Autopsy.

He knew the process included the removal and weighing of the organs which, if Mr Lamb cared to look, would be in a tightly-sealed bag somewhere around James's ankles. He didn't.

Mr Lamb lifted the shroud up, covered over the deceased accountant, flicked the torch off, and slid the drawer closed.

Konstantin tried the first door. Locked. Knew then that they all would be. Found the one he wanted. The shiny brass name plate read 'Coroner'. Picks rattled the tumblers and he was in. The room was sparsely decorated. Desk, computer screen, chair, bookshelves. Small window high in the wall, which would allow almost no meaningful illumination on even the brightest of days. A couple of medical certificates beneath it, a degree and a doctorate. Several pictures. The person who inhabited this office was meticulous. Very likely they'd spot the slightest element that was out of place.

He raised his mobile phone, took three photos. The flash was a harsh, washing-powder white. Satisfied the images showed everything in the room, he entered. Konstantin drew out the chair, booted up computer and printer. Turned on the screen and the room lit up.

Whilst the operating system was loading, Konstantin crossed to the bookshelf and glanced over the spines. All medical journals. He pulled one down, flicked through it. Just as dull on the inside as the outside. He put it back, ensured it lined up exactly.

He shook his head when Windows dropped in without the need to enter a password. Meticulous, highly qualified, but still naive and stupid.

Banana-thick fingers rattled the keys, brought up James' file. He ran a digit down the screen, tapped at the words he wanted. Konstantin slid the mouse over the print option and the pages spat out.

Time to go. PC off, chair under desk. Before he exited Konstantin compared the photo on his mobile against the office layout. Perfect. Door closed and into the passage. Locked it again.

He only had to wait a few moments before Mr Lamb was at his side. He nodded, raised the print-outs, slid the folded paper into his jacket.

The pair went back out through the same window. There was still no-one around, but it remained very early in the morning, well before dawn.

Mr Lamb paused, listened. He couldn't hear a thing. Satisfactory. It had taken them all of twenty minutes to be in and out.

Not bad for ageing men, he thought.

For the thousandth time, Frank wondered how he'd managed to get himself in this position. Not the specific one he was striking now – nonchalant, leaning against a tree and smoking (i.e. cool). No, where he was stuck as a grass to the copper.

In the early days, he'd simply been happy to be in the gang. The ordering around hadn't bothered Frank. Best mates with the boss, making money without trying too hard, able to throw his weight around without fear of retribution, and the birds loved him for it. It had been enough. But then, eventually, it wasn't.

Frank didn't know precisely why or when he'd become dissatisfied, it had sort of sneaked up on him. Perhaps it was as the gang grew in significance and his best mate became his aloof commander-in-chief. Perhaps it was the end of the late night parties. Or the secrets, complex negotiations and deals done without him. He didn't really know. Maybe some, maybe all. Most likely it was the steroids. They'd changed the boss no end.

The final clincher, though, had been the argument. Frank had ballsed something up. Nothing major. A few years ago, Stevie would have laughed about it. They both would have. Gone and got drunk, shagged some girls. But not this time.

Stevie lost his rag. Made it clear Frank was just hired muscle, expendable like the rest. Suddenly their shared past was an irrelevance.

Frank had known straight away who was approaching him, was able to spot bacon a mile off. Plenty of experience with the bastards. It wasn't unusual for the pigs to attempt to turn assumed lawbreakers after an arrest. Hell, it was *expected*. Normally, he'd have given the copper the usual middle digit salute and walked off laughing, knowing there wasn't a fucking thing the police could pull him for. But when this one had come to him, not in a cell or an interview room, but on the street, his street, he was primed and ready to rupture.

It also wasn't that the copper was a mad bastard. That came with the territory for undercover operatives. Inhabiting an alternative identity for months, maybe years. A second skin. Crazy. Instead, Frank had recognised a madness deep behind the eyes. Not just a glimmer, either. A full-on fucking psychosis. The sort that made your hackles rise, made ordinary people want to piss themselves and run.

But Frank was drawn to it like a moth to a flame. He'd met crazy coppers before, but this one was something else. Dominance, yes. Brutality, yes. Lunacy, no. It'd intrigued Frank. Wondered if it was something he could use.

There hadn't been a promise of money. Frank had or could take anything he wanted, when he wanted it. No suggestion of a reduced sentence. Frank knew he'd get off anyway. He had the best legal eagle in the South East in his pocket.

Actually, the inducement had been more powerful than all of the other offers added together. The chance to take down his boss. To attain power. Real power. What he'd always craved, but never quite achieved. On the cusp, although not over the edge.

Frank had played the game and refused the first advance, but nevertheless stuffed the proffered phone number into his pocket. Then, a sufficiently restrained week later, he'd dug it out, called, arranged a meet.

And then it had all started. Did he regret it? Yes. And no.

He felt caught between two resolute objects. To run up against Stevie? By choice? Very bad if it was ever discovered. So Frank just had to ensure the boss never learned about what he was up to. Until it was too late, of course.

And then there was the copper. A right control freak. Frank knew restraint, once applied, could only be taken away via one process – extinction. So the copper had to get it in the end as well. So, for now at least, the only way was forwards. Whether he liked it or not.

He sighed heavily, checked his watch. Luminous hands showed the copper was late.

Again.

It was just for fucking show. He took another powerful draw on his fag. Big lungs for a big man. He flicked the burnt-out butt, watched the orange spark arc through the air. He pulled the packet out from his inside pocket, stuck another cancer stick in the downturned corner of his mouth and flicked the lighter.

"Disgusting habit," the voice said.

Frank tried very hard not to show his surprise. He hadn't heard any movement, yet the copper was standing right next to him. The flame of his lighter still burned.

"Yeah, well. My choice," Frank said, tone hard as flint. He lit up. Didn't want to show surprise.

A dry laugh. "One of the few you've left."

Frank sucked hard on the cigarette. He knew this was just a ploy to fuck with his head.

"Yeah, whatever."

"You're being rude, Frank."

"Uh?"

"It's normal to invite guests to partake in whatever undertaking is at hand."

"What are you on about?"

Sigh. "Give me a fucking cigarette."

Frank's fists tightened. He could *feel* the grin spreading across the copper's face. Manipulative bastard. Well, it wouldn't work.

"You should have just asked." Frank passed the packet over, heard the familiar rustle.

"Lighter?"

Frank flicked the wheel, watched the flame burst into life, desperate to shove it into the copper's hair and warm his hands from the cranial inferno.

He realised the copper hadn't given the fag packet back. Shrugged. Had hundreds at home anyway, but it was the repeated demonstration of power that rankled.

"Don't worry, Frank. Soon you'll be free of us both," said the copper. The grin was in place again. Frank could see the white teeth as the fag went up to the copper's lips.

He grunted. "Top fucking event that'll be."

"But not today or tomorrow."

They stood together, huffing smoke into the air. An odd acceptance of fate hanging. It was the copper who broke the silence, of course.

"So ... tell me. What's going on in the world of Stevie Oakhill?"

Frank told.

"It was murder," Mr Lamb said. He was driving the hire car from scene of corpse. Scene of crime would be visited later. "Puncture mark in the neck. Hard to see, but unmistakable once observed."

"Was not in autopsy notes."

"Interesting. What about the toxicology report?"

Konstantin shook his head. "Inconclusive."

"They'll settle on death by misadventure then."

"Probably."

"Definitely, I'd say. All the evidence points in that direction."

They drove on in silence, all the while Mr Lamb wondering why someone would kill James Hollowman. Determine the why, and the answer to the most important question, who, would follow. The murderer had to be a person of influence.

But then again, it usually was.

The First Betrayal

I decide I want a coffee, need it to stay awake, it's so late. Risk-taker that I am, I make one. Whilst it's brewing (we don't do instant shit here), I listen to the rest of Gowan's monologue over the mobile's speaker:

"What do you want?" That's me, sounding whiny.
"I wish you to look into James' death."
"Why?"
"Because we need to know what happened?"
"We? There's no *we* in it, mate. Besides, I don't want to be a hero. I gave that crap up. It didn't get me anything other than a shitload of trouble."
"I'll make it worth your while."
"How? Live people struggle to get credit these days, never mind the dearly departed." I smile for a second time. I'm still quite pleased with that one.
"As I said, I put my affairs in order, so I'm not entirely without means."
"I also might get dead."
"I doubt it, Mr Brodie."
"Tell that to your mate James."
Gowan glared at me, wanting to argue, but aware I was a couple of moves from checkmate and out.
"I know your finances are weak." On life support, actually.
"I'm not too badly off," I lie.
"I've seen your bank balance. Your outgoings far outweigh your income. In fact your income is virtually zero."
I'm amazed he knows this.
"So?"
"So, I'll pay you handsomely to find out what happened to James."
Gowan had tugged a pile of notes out of his pocket that you could have beaten somebody to death with and handed them over. At least I could buy petrol to get home now, I'd thought.

"That's just a down payment," he says. "And if Gordon is to blame, then we'll bring him down together. Consider the opportunity for retribution."

He didn't give me chance to think, stood up. Little bugger had been sitting on something and his arse was totally dry. He handed that to me as well. A supermarket bag. Not a cheap one, oh no. It's 'For Life', apparently. Which proves he has more money than sense.

"Thanks," I say. "Bit late though."

I'd stood, showed him my cod wet backside. He'd displayed no interest in the damp state of my trousers, pressed the carrier into my hands. I'd looked within. Paper. With words and numbers on.

"How do I keep in touch?" I ask.

I'd dropped the wedge of cash into the bag to huddle with the documents.

"I'll call you," he says. "The less you know about me, the better."

I turn the voice recorder off. The sound of a dead man speaking. And a seagull. It's evidence, really. I look again in the bag, take the money out, rummage around. Find, buried at the bottom, a USB stick. Gowan hadn't mentioned that.

I pull it out, contemplate it momentarily, then shove it in my pocket when my phone beeps. It's a text message that says, "Hi! I'm Lucy! Gray told you about me. Want to meet tomorrow? Then text me! XXX"

Not the best first impression I've ever been given. At least it was all spelt correctly. None of this shorthand crap. I sigh. Fucking Gray. Initially, I consider replying with a no, but then I remember she knows something about Dredge.

I slowly tap out a reply. "O ... K ..."

An instant later she replies. "Great! Let me know when and where."

I decide I'll respond tomorrow. I stand up, turn the light off.

It's dark now. Good.

Just me and my memories. Not so good.

Instead of the coffee, I open another can of beer, get ready to throw the empty at my depression.

An Apparent Crime Scene

"This it?" Mr Lamb asked.

"Da. Pretty obvious, is not?" Konstantin replied. He pointed at the criss-crossed police tape with the kebab he'd insisted they stop for. It was mainly grease, chillies, and some meat of dubious source stuffed into a stale, dough-like substance unlikely to be bread. A great gob of fat chose that moment to drip onto the floor.

Mr Lamb eyed the slick patch with a modicum of distaste. The Russian shrugged a shoulder, then threw the kebab over it to land somewhere in the pitch darkness behind. Mr Lamb heard the splat, wondered how far the sauce had spread.

"Coming?" Konstantin asked, but didn't wait for an answer.

The strip of blue and white plastic was no barrier to entry, a couple of sharp tugs and it was just more litter on the ground. Konstantin pushed at the door, which squeaked for good measure.

Mr Lamb would have known they were in a lavatory, simply by the aroma of disinfectant cut through with a hint of piss. That the public facility was in a dimly-lit park surrounded by bushes and trees on the border between two towns was just incidental. And bad planning.

Other than being a crime scene, it was in all ways identical to every other men's room he'd ever been in – damp, graffitied and cold. The space opened up, after an obligatory formica division, on Mr Lamb's left. Three urinals, two sinks and two stalls, neither with doors (and no toilet paper either, he would bet).

"According to the police report, he was found in the far cubicle," Mr Lamb said, shining his pencil torch into the black depths. A seagull blinked in the harsh light. It skittered across the floor and cowered under a sink.

"Fucking rats," Konstantin spat. He'd hated them since first arriving in the UK.

Mr Lamb shook his head. "Come on, we haven't got time to waste."

The beam illuminated the stall – lavatory with seat up and toilet-roll holder (empty as predicted), with a glory hole beside it. The walls were picked out in white tiles to the rear, lewd scrawls to right and left. And that was it.

Functional, rough, basic.

The external door squeaked. Mr Lamb and Konstantin pirouetted in unison. A man in leather jacket and jeans stopped dead in his tracks. Goggled at the pair, then at the bird.

"Er, hello," he said. Mr Lamb wasn't sure whether he was speaking to them or the flying vermin.

"I take this," Konstantin said.

"Be my guest." Mr Lamb waved the Russian on.

Konstantin closed the gap, got into the guy's personal space to see if it bothered him. It didn't.

"You're quite forward, big man. I've not seen you here before," he said.

"And?" Konstantin replied.

The guy stretched out, attempting to touch Konstantin with fingertips, but before he could make contact, Konstantin span him around and drove his arm up his back. He squealed, stood on tiptoes to assuage the pain.

Mr Lamb quickly searched him. Found a wallet, checked the credit cards within, replaced it.

"Let Mr Brown go."

"No attempt to touch, da?" Konstantin said.

"Ah! Fuck, yes! Let go of me, you maniac!" Brown squealed a bit more as Konstantin pushed the limb an inch further upwards.

"Konstantin," Mr Lamb said gently. "Play nicely."

The Russian gave an extra tweak, then released. Brown lurched back. Started rubbing at his shoulder, irate expression on his features.

"Are you crazy? You could have broken my arm!"

Konstantin shook his head. "If I wanted, it already done."

Mr Lamb stepped between the exit and Brown, said, "I assume you come here often?"

Immediately, Brown switched from angry to suspicious. His posture stiffened, any pain forgotten. "For a piss, yes," he said. "But not for a few days, as it's been closed off."

"Right," Mr Lamb said. He looked at Brown's wedding band, then into his eyes. "Your wife knows about your extra-curricular activities, then?"

Brown's shoulders slumped. "No, she doesn't." At least he had the good grace to colour.

"Have you seen this person before?" Mr Lamb raised a photo to eye level, shone his torch on the image. Brown glanced at it.

"No."

"Look again," Konstantin said.

Brown flicked his eyes from Mr Lamb to Konstantin and then down. He stared at James's face, an official picture from a Dredge Industries press release.

"*No.*"

"Are you certain?" Mr Lamb said. "This is very important."

"How many times do I have to answer in the negative before you get the message? I've never seen the person in this photo here or anywhere else that I may have frequented!"

Mr Lamb scrutinised Brown, saw nothing in his pupils to say he was lying. Eventually, he said, "Thank you."

"Now, may I go please? I'm pretty pressed for time."

Konstantin and Mr Lamb parted. Brown sidled between, watching them both warily. He went into the end stall, where James had been found. Mr Lamb shook his head at the Russian.

"None of our concern," he said.

The pair left the seagull and Brown to their respective business.

Outside Konstantin sighed, frustrated. "Told you, nothing to see."

"Not necessarily. Could you imagine James coming to a place like this?"

Konstantin shrugged. "No, but I not really know him."

"So I'll ask someone who does."

"You do that on own."

Mr Lamb gave a slight nod of agreement, even though it was too dark for Konstantin to see. "Later today, though. Let's go."

Frank was hot-wired, felt like his brain was on fire. Since meeting the copper, he'd hit the town hard with the boys to try and blow the strain away. Lager, chasers, cocaine – they'd barely touched the sides. Even Squirrel, not the brightest spark in the fire at the best of times, had noticed his fucked-up mood.

The night really went to shit when Frank started a fight with a couple of lads. He'd felt up their girlfriends, just to provoke a reaction. A slap he'd expected as a minimum, would have been pleased with that. But when the situation descended into a full-blown scrum with bottles and chairs arcing over their heads, he was fucking delighted.

Frank made to pile in, but the others were wiser. It took three of them to drag him outside.

"Coppers'll be here soon," Squirrel hissed. "They'll bang you up if you give 'em the excuse."

Frank struggled some more. Squirrel struck below the belt, hit the weak spot – his ego – said, "Think about it. You're a face. Big target for them to take down. Don't give 'em the excuse."

It worked. Realising he couldn't be picked up by the police at a time like this, the tornado mood dropped to a breeze. He shook off Squirrel's restraining hand, straightened his leather, and stalked away from the pub.

The Merc was parked across two bays by the harbour. He tugged the parking ticket from under a wiper, tossed it into the water.

"Want me to drive?" Squirrel asked.

"Fuck, no."

Just as Frank started the engine, his mobile rang. He stabbed at the keypad to answer it. "What?"

A moment's silence on the other end. Then, "You disrespectin' me, Frank?"

Shit, Frank thought. He kicked himself for not checking the caller ID first. Stevie.

"No, boss. Just been a rough day."

Silence again, then, "Get your arse in here now. I need to speak to you."

"Boss, it's 1.30am."

"So fuckin' what? Let's get this straight. Here. Chop fuckin' chop. Talk."

The line went dead.

"Out," Frank said.

"Eh?" Squirrel said. "What you on about, boss?"

"I said get out the fucking car. Stevie wants to see me."

"Shit, boss, can't you drop us home? Getting a taxi will be a bitch this time of night."

"Not my problem." Frank turned to stare into Squirrel's eyes. Even sitting down, he was a foot taller and three feet harder.

Squirrel blinked, popped the passenger door open. Tyrone and Barnie followed. The moment they were out, Frank slammed the car into reverse, aimed the car in the right direction, drove away in a plume of smoke.

There was no way Frank could make it in fifteen minutes. He knew it, Stevie knew it. Like the copper, it was all just mind-fuck games. Frank slammed his palm into the steering wheel several times in frustration.

This had to stop. Very soon. He couldn't take it any longer.

Twenty five hard driving minutes later, Frank pulled onto the long gravel driveway, eventually stopped outside the house. He killed the lights and sat in the dark for a moment, collecting his wits.

His head was still bollocksed with the drink, drugs and fight. It wouldn't do to lose it now. Not in the lion's den. He smoked a fag in huge breaths, the nicotine oddly calming. Felt his heart rate slow.

He walked up to the front door. Locked. That was a first.

Frank growled, raised a fist, banged it on the wood. It opened a moment later and he stepped inside. A couple of thugs he hadn't seen before patted him down, removed his gun.

"Fuck's this?" Frank bridled.

"New rules," he was told.

"Do you know who I am?"

Shrug. "Same for everyone."

"Fuck's sake."

"He's in the library. And he's not in a good mood."

"Great."

Frank entered, flopped onto the hard chair destined for guests. Stevie Oakhill sat the other side of the huge glass desk, in the semi-shade of a lamp, writing, apparently oblivious to Frank.

The only other light source was the moon that shone in through the large picture window that opened onto manicured lawn, groomed flower beds and defined topiary. Frank thought it poncy. Another sign Stevie had gone soft. The man even covered up his tattoos these days. Including the first proper one they'd got as teenagers together – the devil for Stevie, dripping fangs for Frank. Both on their left arms. Defining moments in their lives. Worn with pride. Or used to be.

Although you wouldn't know it to look at Stevie now, when they'd been at school together, he was the weed, the one who always got picked on. Little Stevie was the kid that never fit in, the one that was different to everyone else. Like a glove with four fingers, what good was he? His accent marked him straight away. He wasn't from the same town, never mind the same estate. That was bad fucking news anywhere, never mind Hull.

But Stevie always stood up for himself, gave at least as good as he got in a fight. He'd been a tough little bastard. Hard as a nut. Eventually, the bullies got the message, left him alone, shifted onto softer targets that didn't kick back.

Somehow, the circumstances were a dim memory now. Stevie had entered Frank's sphere and they'd fallen in together. Brains and brawn. They'd proved a powerful pairing, quickly starting to make cash, growing in influence. Selling fags, beer, porn videos, even a few drugs. Anything to turn a fast buck. Their success enthralled others, drew them in and the gang grew ...

"Good to see you, Frank," Stevie broke into his thoughts. "Can I get you a drink?"

"No thanks. I've been puttin' it away all night."

"Unlike you to turn down a freebie, but suit yourself."

"What do you want, Stevie?"

The Steroid sighed. "We've a problem. Someone's been talking."

Frank's heart turned into an icicle, whilst the pit of his stomach boiled. He'd heard Stevie voice this thought before, but he couldn't help worrying. He forced himself not to show any emotion. Trouble was, Stevie was total calm. Usually the time to be the most worried, when emotion was buried under a rock. Frank's apprehension eased up a notch.

"Who?"

"Not sure, but something's going on. We lost another shipment today."

"To the Chechens again?"

"Yes, and they shot the guard. Took half his head off."

In the last couple of weeks, a new gang had been muscling in on their operation. Hitting cargoes, stopping trade, beating up pimps. Overall, shit for business. The armed guards were a reaction from Stevie. He didn't like the idea of the load being pulled by a copper, finding a weapon, questions asked. But he didn't have any alternative, the pickings were too rich.

"What do you want me to do about it?"

"The driver's bagged up in the barn outside. Probably had fuck all to do with it, but we need to set an example, so take him out into the marshes, see if he does knows anything, then get rid. And make it fucking messy."

"Who's coming with me?"

Stevie looked at him, a question mark on his brow. "No-one. This is all for you. Special treat."

Frank didn't like it, but knew better than to argue. This was a test.

Stevie took silence for acquiescence, said, "Good. So, what happened with Mr Gowan?"

"He's fish food somewhere in the North Sea. I drowned him like a kitten. No bother at all."

"Pity, but ah well. Loose ends always need tying up. And the reporter?"

"He was a no-show."

"Gowan didn't talk to him?"

Frank shook his head. "He kicked around on the beach for ten or fifteen minutes waiting, then I got bored and did for him."

Stevie laughed, short, sharp and empty of humour. "First bit of good news I've heard all day. I assume you going to sort Brodie out eventually?"

"Erm, no, boss. Why would we? He's a nobody."

"Loose ends, Frank. Always tie them up."

"Can't go knocking off reporters, boss. Even washed up ones. They're like coppers: kill one, more appear."

"Maybe you're right, Frank."

"It won't be a problem, boss. Promise."

"I'll hold you to that. Now fuck off and deal with the driver then."

Frank didn't need telling twice. He fucked off.

Stevie sat still as a statue once Frank had left, thinking hard. In recent weeks, a stable and successful business had gone haywire.

Fucking Chechens. Stevie hadn't told Frank about the message. Didn't see the point.

Deal, or they'd take the lot.

He turned the lamp off and stared at the pale celestial body that grinned down at him.

Felt like howling.

Accountable

Four Days Ago

The next day yawns. I still populate my orphaned chair. I wake early because:

> One, it's light.
> Two, there aren't any curtains to dim the room.
> Three, there's no rail to hang the curtains from.

I stand, stretch, crunch. A moment of anxiety that I've put my back out, but realise it's a beer can underfoot, rather than my bones. There's an interesting stack of tinnies next to my chair that I don't recall constructing.

That's a couple more brain cells murdered, then.

Nicotine withdrawal kicks in. The fag packet's in my shirt pocket. I pull a little death stick out and light it. By the time I've gone upstairs, had a piss, neglected to wash my hands and return, the fag is three quarters gone.

I brew some coffee, dump a decent measure into a chipped cup. No milk (or fridge), so it's black. Retreat to my chair, spill some onto Gowan's file. I pick it up and wipe the liquid off with my sleeve. A proportion of the ink smears. Ah well, it's still legible and not too much is on my shirt.

I start to skim-read. The majority of the text I already know, basic background stuff and as meaty as a veggie burger. The bulk of the content is made up of numbers. They mean less than fuck-all to me, but must to someone.

After five minutes, I reach the end. Read Gowan's note again, wonder what's on the USB stick. I rise, retrieve my laptop from the boot of the Shit Machine. I keep everything of value in there. Who's going to think of breaking into such a piece of crap?

Once the operating system has loaded, I push the USB drive into the requisite slot. A folder pops up. Within are two documents:

'Info.'
'Read Me First.'

So I do. It simply says, 'Within is everything you need. The analogue version isn't the full story.'

Go onto the next page and there's simply … the name of a bank. Eight numbers. Six numbers split into pairs with dashes.

An account number and sort code, then.

Nothing else. No identity of the holder. Very puzzling.

I download the files onto my laptop, return it to the boot along with the cash. Get a shower. Leave the bag of paper in the living room. It's valueless after all.

A Pointless Murder

Frank tamped down the soil, tossed some branches and leaves over the shallow grave. He brushed at the mud covering his trousers, wiped the sweat from his brow. It wasn't easy digging packed dirt, frozen solid by the low temperatures.

The despatch itself had been pathetically easy. The driver was tiny. A shivering mess, tightly bound with coils of rope, hooded with a hessian sack, cowering in the corner of the garage. He hadn't seen the knockout punch coming.

Frank had then bundled the cataleptic form into the Merc's boot, driven for half an hour until he was well away from Stevie's house and in some dense woodland. Parked the car, put the headlights on full beam, started digging.

The driver was alert by the time Frank came to get him. He wriggled like a caterpillar, all energy and no progress. Another punch, a bit more dragging until the man was in the hole, then a bullet to the head. Hit him a few times with a spade.

Compassionate yet effective.

No point torturing the guy, because Frank knew full well he had no information to deliver. But then so did Stevie.

Frank wasn't happy. It had been many a year since he'd been required to be both executioner and cleaner. This was what the lower echelons were employed for – get their hands dirty, take the risks. Figured he was getting old. Drinking, murdering, and the early hours were increasingly getting to him.

He sat on the car bonnet, lit a fag, watched the sky turn from grey to gold. Thought about the next steps.

The reporter, Brodie, there to create a messy front whilst Frank worked constructively in the background. The stuff that Gowan had handed over, Frank knew should be retrieved. Once Brodie had taken a good look. Couldn't allow the copper to know there was more information than agreed within the package, but figured he had a few days yet.

Two potential problems, though. Stevie suspected there was an informer inside the gang. Someone needed to take the fall. He had an idea of who, just not the how.

And those fucking Chechens. They were a wild card he could do without. No controlling them. Who knew what those mad bastards would do?

Frank shrugged. Something would pop up. It always did. Chucked his spent fag-end, dumped the spade in the boot, left the driver at peace.

Wake Me Up

The funeral is today, specifically now. Fittingly, the atmosphere is as black as a nun's cowl. Rain looks a certainty.

Hollowman is being sent to balance the great ledger in the sky. Which is about as plausible as there being a place called Heaven where angels play harps, or seventy virgins frolic, or whatever version of bullshit you've been told exists.

I don't have an invite to the ceremony and crashing it doesn't feel right, so I kick my heels in the crematorium car park whilst they're inside. I smoke a couple of fags, sigh a lot, take the odd hit from my hip flask. For warmth, of course.

I pull at my too-tight shirt collar, struggling to remember the last time I wore a tie. By the constricting size of the suit I'm wearing, pulled down from the loft earlier in the day, I reckon it's several years ago. I wonder if it's the get-up I wore to my wedding.

Half a cigarette packet later, the mourners file out the back door, into the memorial garden. A decent sized crowd mill around the flower arrangements for a few minutes, reading the notes.

But people usually don't like to hang around – it reminds them one day it'll be their turn. However, there's a balance in the timing. Too quickly, they appear callous, too long, they appear ghoulish.

A bit of drizzle is all the excuse needed. With the first splash, an old bloke makes a break for it, opens the metaphorical floodgates. In moments, a less than subtle headlong dash ensues and a queue of cars snakes along the drive as demand outstrips supply.

I manage to position the Shit Machine behind the not-so grieving widow. I'm not saying she looks happy (far from it), but she's not a mess of tears either. Quite cute, actually. A striking blonde. She looks tough, though. Hard as nails.

I'm taking a calculated risk, anticipating there will be some sort of wake. If it's in a public place, I'm in. And vice versa. For once, good fortune prevails. Blondie pulls up outside a hostelry on a tight bend overlooking the harbour. Except you can't see anything remotely describable as a view, because the weather is now shitting cats and dogs. Which made for interesting driving without operational windscreen wipers.

The guests run inside. I park up, well away from everyone else, pull my jacket over my head, and run like fuck.

"I'm so sorry for your loss," I say, shaking Blondie's dry hand (nicely manicured nails, smooth skin) with a damp palm. It's never felt natural, this. I can't go for the standard male competitive death grip, but it's not in me to offer a pathetic squeeze either.

Fair fucks to her, though, because she gives mine a wringing that a mangle would be proud of.

"Thank you Mr ... ? Sorry, I don't believe we've met before?"

"You're right. We haven't. I'm David Brodie."

"The reporter?"

"Yes." I'm somewhat amazed she's heard my name. "Long-lost fame?"

"You wrote the short article in the paper last week."

"So I did." Shit, I'd forgotten about that.

"I expect you'll understand that I won't be making a statement."

"No problem, Mrs Hollowman. I completely understand." I'm not interested in words, I want to see faces. But I verbalise, "I'll leave you in peace."

She grabs my arm as I move away, says, "It's Emily. I can't stop you being here, but I'd appreciate it if you didn't trouble my guests." She smiles in a baring of teeth kind of way, turns her back on me. I'm in no doubt that I'll be wearing my balls for earrings should I ignore her wishes.

I lift a drink from a passing tray (it's being carried by a waitress, no magic here) and down it in one. The bubbles go up my nose and I snort. There's a brief lull in conversation whilst everyone looks at me.

I wave a hand at them, in case someone is considering applying mouth-to-mouth. A second later and I'm forgotten, as is my resuscitation from the edge of death. I snag another beverage, but take this one at a little more of a refined pace. Leaning against a beam and standing up a couple of steps, I can see across the whole bar.

Most of the grievers are decked out in grey suits, pinstripes, long woollen coats. Clearly accountants, clearly wealthy. And it's an almost entirely male soiree. I don't know if that's because of James' alleged sexual inclinations, or that business is a largely male affair. It's probably both, but who cares?

Then, in he comes.

Gordon Dredge, followed by an ox of a man (as strong and intelligent by the lean of his features) and a gust of wind. Dredge's companion is as wide as a house. Fucking fat would be an understatement. The bodyguard scans the room. As they pass me, I hear Dredge say, "You can leave me now, Piles. I won't do anything stupid."

"I'll be sticking to you like shit, Gordon, don't you worry," Piles growls.

Interesting.

Enter Dredge, Stage Left

Mr Lamb had gone to the memorial service without Konstantin. By his sheer bulk, he was sometimes simply too memorable, whichever guise he adopted.

The last to enter the chapel, he'd stayed at the rear whilst the ceremony was proceeding, and was the first to exit into the garden at its conclusion. Keeping his face turned away from the mourners, Mr Lamb surveyed the plaques of people he'd never met, dead years before him, some not much older than he was now. He felt a momentary finger of mortality, but cremated it as quickly as it surfaced.

He knew where the wake was due to be held, and arrived in good time. Drifting with the throng, he went unnoticed. As he sipped carbonated water, Mr Lamb unobtrusively skimmed the bar area, listening to, but never joining in, the conversations.

They were largely bland and almost all commercially orientated. The brief lull while a scruffy man choked momentarily was a welcome, but all too brief, diversion. His curiosity peaked when Gordon Dredge finally entered. The obvious minder was an interesting touch. It seemed a little excessive to him.

Mr Lamb lingered a few feet back and eavesdropped on Dredge's discussions. Absolutely irrelevant. He suppressed a sigh. That was how it went sometimes. After precisely an hour, he decided it was time to make his excuses and depart. Mr Lamb found the widow.

"Leaving so soon?" Emily said.

"Yes, unfortunately. I have another engagement."

"That's a pity. This is so much fun, isn't it?"

"I'm sorry for your loss."

"No, I should apologise." She sighed. "It's been a strange day. I don't usually do flippant remarks. I hope you got what you wanted?"

"Not quite. I was hoping we could talk. Not here, naturally."

"I'll be at my office later if you want to pop in." Emily handed a business card over.

Mr Lamb nodded.

"Thank you for coming," she said.

"My pleasure. I'll see you in due course."

As he was walking up the short flight of steps to the exit, Mr Lamb heard someone say, "Escaping already? Very smart."

Mr Lamb paused, locked eyes with the speaker. They were bloodshot, rimmed with black. Messy hair, not stylish, just unkempt. Grubby, wrinkled clothes in an array of styles, tie askew and top shirt-button undone. Hastily thrown on then, Mr Lamb guessed. He could smell the nicotine and the desultory mint freshener on his breath.

The reporter, Brodie. Best not to reply. Mr Lamb didn't, stepped out from one squall into another.

Trouble In Paradise

I'd watched watch Dredge work the room until I couldn't stomach any more. Blondie had kept glancing at me, making sure I wasn't making a nuisance of myself, so eventually I'd covertly pocketed a couple of glasses and sodded off out of there.

I sit in the car now, wet again, and think back to when I saw Dredge do a television interview. It was only a little over a year ago and formed part of my research. He'd been on some panel, facing an audience with an adjudicator sat dead centre. Dredge looked fat, successful and arrogant. His performance utterly confirmed the perception.

A female MP, the youngest in the Government at the time, was seated next to Dredge. She didn't look happy about it. He'd barely bothered to keep the deep sneer off his face throughout the event.

But then the pair got into a heated debate over a question posed by someone in the audience. I can't remember precisely what the subject was – the economic recovery, I think.

Interestingly, Dredge fought not to look directly at the woman. She kept trying to engage him, literally leaning right over and looking into his face. But all the time, Dredge steadfastly stared forward or down at the table surface. Like she, and her opinion, was entirely valueless. Which to him, they were.

To be fair to the woman, she kept her temper in check. If anything, she laughed at the fat bastard. Even the audience booed. And Dredge didn't give a shit. A multi-millionaire from a privileged background, he was correct, regardless of the facts. Was his God-given right to act how he fucking liked, because that's what he'd always done and always would.

Today, he's still a smug bastard. That fundamental fact will never change, but something was different. The presence of the antagonistic bodyguard was one, the deferential nature another. And, also, it seemed like his clothes didn't quite fit – his tailored suit hung off him.

Clearly all is not well in the land of Dredge, and that pleases me greatly.

It's another hour before Dredge departs the soiree. He staggers slightly, clearly the worse for wear. Piles sneers, shakes his head, doesn't hide his distaste for the man. I'd guess he also isn't a fully paid-up member of Dredge's fan club. They walk past. I put my hand over my face. Neither appears to notice me.

Piles unlocks the green Bentley parked a few spaces in front of the Shit Machine, clambers none too elegantly into the driver's seat. Dredge fumbles with the car door-handle, like it's unfamiliar to him. Eventually, he cracks the code and falls inside. Piles tears away, throwing Dredge around like dirty clothes in a washing machine.

I follow, struggling to keep up with the big-engined monster. Piles treats the Bentley like it's a dodgem. He's aggressive, accelerates rapidly, cuts everyone up. Thankfully, the traffic is crap.

A frantic half-hour later, I wait outside Dredge's place. 'Nice' is about the weakest possible word to describe. 'Grand' is about halfway there. It's a Georgian mansion with a tree-lined driveway and acre upon acre of land to muck about on, so large it possesses its own postcode.

Frankly, it wouldn't do for me. I'm lazy. Just more grass to cut, trees to tend etc. Although, I guess, he can easily afford hired hands. He bloody needs them to look after this gaff.

The exclusive location means, though, that I can't park anywhere near. Not legally, anyway.

My bonnet is up, hazards blinking on-off. The Shit Machine is half on the grass, half in the B road that runs adjacent to his property. I'm therefore an unnatural traffic-calming event, although the drivers that go past me look less than relaxed by the colour of both their language and faces. Water off a turkey's back.

However, I reckon it won't be long before the Old Bill turn up. I'm probably on a radio traffic report somewhere by now.

I lean against the rear bumper, facing towards the drive. I've created a bit of a problem – busy roads aren't conducive to the car chase process. However, as I smoke a fag and shrug apologetically (not meaning a millimetre of the shoulder movement) to another meathead on the way to an early grave from high blood pressure, I see the Bentley negotiating the drive.

I lift the small but powerful binoculars, which I cleverly have in my hand for just this event, up to my eyes. They're even focused properly. How do you like that?

Uh-huh, it's Dredge in the back seat, Piles driving. The fag ends up in the hedge, the binos on the back seat. The bonnet's down with a large bang in one fluid movement. I hold my hand up to stop the arse trying to squeeze past my car, yank open my door, kick the engine into action.

I keep my eyes on the rear-view. Good luck – the Bentley turns left and towards moi. I turn my hazards off. Within a minute, the Bentley is sliding past me, and I drop off the verge a couple of cars back from my target.

99 Red Balloons

Today was Lucy's birthday. Not that you'd know it. Celebrations were minimal by choice. She'd struggled to cheer about anything mundane since the day her brother had died.

The cards were lined up on the windowsill. Lucy counted them, a process that took no time at all, literally. One. Two.

A picture of a dog with big, sad eyes (from mother). A ballerina twirling (Gray, of course). Her one birth parent and an old school friend were the sum of her social contact.

Is this it? she wondered. *I'm only twenty eight. Am I destined to be alone forever?*

She looked at her phone again. No texts. She put it back down on the bed. Fucking hell. It was her birthday, she should be getting drunk at least! Before her nerve went, Lucy snatched up her mobile and punched in his number ...

"I'm taking a big fucking risk here," Frank said. "Meeting you like this. If Stevie found out ..."

The copper shrugged. "Tough shit. That's the risk you snitches take. Besides, we both know your boss is otherwise engaged right now."

"I ain't a fucking snitch!" he roared.

"Keep your voice down, you idiot."

Frank kicked at a stone, watched it fly into the sea. They'd met at a remote bay, gone down to the water's edge, away from prying ears and eyes.

"What the fuck do you want, then?" Frank hissed. He was desperate for a fag, to warm his body up, but made himself wait. There was no way he was showing weakness in front of the copper.

"I need regular updates from you. Every day. To keep me in the loop. Everything will be coming to a head soon. It has to."

"Nothing's happened. 'sides, it's difficult to get to a phone. Stevie's easily suspicious. He sliced some fella last year 'cos he suspected he was ratting on us. Unlucky bastard had his guts in his hands all the while he bled out."

"Very nice, but I don't give a shit."

"'You will, if I get caught, 'cos you'd be coming down with me. So it's in your interest to keep me sweet, mate."

There was a momentary silence. The air between them was cold and hard. The waves battered the shoreline to their backs.

The copper spoke very quietly. "If you ever threaten me again, I'll ensure Stevie gets to hear of you playing both sides of the game. You'll be all on your own, because I'll be miles away and completely untouchable."

Frank blinked. Didn't believe the threat. But was scared of it nevertheless. He gave in, lit a fag, drew hard on it, said through the smoke, "Aye, fucking whatever."

"Good. I'm glad we understand each other."

"Crystal, *mate*."

"I also have an insider feeding me information that may help, so it's important you keep the phone on."

Frank's eyes narrowed. This was front page shit news. "Who is he?"

The copper smiled. "That'll have to remain a clandestine matter, I'm afraid."

"Do you have to sound like such a posh twat all the time?"

The copper delivered a heavy sigh. "My part of the bargain remains the same. Just keep yours and we'll both be in clover."

The copper's mobile rang.

Ryan's Game

My phone rings. That's all it does. No stupid pieces of music or manic voices, just rings. I'm driving and I don't have anything new-fangled, like Bluetooth. I answer, holding it to my ear with a shoulder so I can steer and change gears.

Who says men can't multi-task?

"What?" says I.

"Is that David?" An entirely unfamiliar female voice, young and unsullied by life from the sound of it.

"I couldn't possibly say."

"Oh."

Pause. I negotiate a roundabout in shared silence. The Bentley is still in sight, although Piles has just missed a cyclist by a millimetre.

"Are you still there?" I ask.

"Yes, are you?"

"Of course. This is my phone."

"Right." She seems to accept my stupid comments at face value. She might be all right, this girl, whoever the hell she is. Intelligent women are the curse of lazy men.

"By the way, excuse me for asking, but who is this?"

"Lucy Ryan. Gray should have mentioned me?"

Nope, no idea who you are, love. My memory is shot to shit. I verbalise, "Erm..."

"I sent you a text yesterday?"

"Oh yes, that's right." No it isn't, I still can't remember.

"I'd like to get drunk, please," she says.

Now that takes me by surprise. I could do with something to cheer me up so I reply, "Well, fuck it, why not?"

She laughs with childish glee. I almost change my mind there and then. I should have done. We arrange where to meet, end the call. Mobile ends up on passenger seat.

The rest of the drive is short and uneventful. We arrive at a Michelin starred restaurant. Dredge goes inside. Interestingly, Piles stays in the car, racks his seat back, stretches out for some shut eye.

I wait. Again. Wondering what this Lucy bird is like.

The Last Supper

The waiter pulled out a chair for Gordon Dredge, brushed the seat off, placed a serviette on his lap once installed. It was that sort of restaurant – where nothing was too much bother for the staff.

He was handed a menu. Dredge glanced over it. No prices. If that was an issue to the patron, then they shouldn't have walked in.

It had been far too long since he'd eaten well. Going to fancy places had once been a daily event. He'd thought nothing of spending eye-watering quantities of cash. Amounts that the average family could live on comfortably for a year, gone in a couple of hours. Back then, he hadn't cared. It was one of his well-earned privileges. Not anymore.

Stevie Oakhill was already at the table. His two bodyguards, huge guys in well-tailored, tight fitting suits were adjacent. They looked distinctly out of place, but these days, Oakhill rarely left his fortress, and never without protection.

"Shall I order, Gordie?" Stevie said.

"Fine with me," Dredge replied, signalling a waiter. "Whiskey, dash of mineral water."

"Sir, anything for you?" the waiter asked Oakhill.

"The rest of his mineral water will do fine." Stevie didn't do alcohol. Just pills. "And the taster menu for two."

"Very good, sir."

They sat in silence until the drinks arrived. "Same again," said Dredge, before the glass even touched the table.

Continued silence until Dredge couldn't stand it any longer, burst out and said, "So Steven, to what do I owe this utter displeasure?"

The Steroid smiled thinly. Took a sip of his water. The ice tinkled as he put it back down.

"Why do you think there's a purpose behind everything, Gordie?"

Dredge laughed, loud in the hushed room. Heads turned. "Because there always is, where you're concerned."

"There was the day when I would have said the same of you."

"Touché. However, that was before you put me under house-arrest with that bastard Piles watching my every move."

"You can hardly blame me for that, Gordon."

"Oh, but I can, and I will."

The first course was delivered, a foie gras. Dredge noted that Stevie still only used his fork to eat with. Knives were for stabbing people. Preferably in the back.

"It's rather excellent, isn't it?" Stevie noted.

"I've had better." Dredge shrugged.

"Not bad for a last supper, though, Gordie."

"Is that what this is? Final meal for the condemned man?"

"It's up to you what you call it, Gordie."

Dredge glared at Stevie, who just smiled back. The fine food suddenly tasted like cardboard, the whiskey like piss.

He pushed his plate away, couldn't help himself. "So, when will the deed be done?"

"If, by 'deed', I assume you're asking when we'll finish the job?" Oakhill asked.

Dredge nodded.

"I haven't decided yet. Could be today, could be tomorrow, could be next week. Maybe even a year or two. You'll just have to wait with baited breath, my old friend."

Dredge waved at the waiter, ordered another malt whiskey. A double this time. Twenty five years old.

"Not eating, Gordon?"

"Surprisingly, I've rather lost my appetite."

"Pity, as today you can have whatever you want."

"The only thing I don't understand is, why?" Dredge asked. His stomach was virtually empty and the alcohol was seething through his bloodstream, rushing to his head, making it spin, making him daring.

Oakhill burst out laughing, an explosion of gut-bursting mirth. This time, the whole restaurant stopped to stare. Waiters paused with food half-way to guests' plates, one continued pouring wine until the goblet filled, overflowed. Oakhill paid them no heed.

Eventually, he stopped, wiped a tear from his eye. The restaurant snapped into going about its business again.

"I'm sorry, Gordie, I couldn't keep a straight face any longer. Why would I want to kill you? It'd be all over the news."

"So you were toying with me."

"Always. Just for a giggle."

Dredge's hand tightened around the crystal, so taut it might shatter. Hoped it would, slice an artery and he could bleed out here, take the gratification of his demise away from Oakhill.

Stevie must have read his mind because he reached over, plucked the glass out of his grip.

"I think you've had enough, Gordon." Oakhill sat back, placed the fork on his plate. "So you really want to know why?"

Dredge nodded, his head heavy. It felt like his neck was on the block, Stevie holding the axe, ready to fall.

"You're tainted goods of no value. No-one will do business with you again. Nobody wants to invest in you anymore. You've hoovered up everyone's money and lost it. I've taken all you have, except your ego. So no, I'm not going to kill you. What's going to happen is worse. You'll be a nobody soon, slip further into obscurity. Not a penny to your name. Your face will be forgotten – old news, tomorrow's chip paper. I may throw you a bone every now and again, like this." Oakhill beatifically waved his arm around the restaurant.

"But in a year, you'll be unknown, a tramp living on the streets. You might last two, three years tops. I've a personal bet with myself that you'll end it. Throw yourself under a bus, probably. Or off a high building. Or drink yourself to death. Either way, by your own hand, not mine."

Dredge was lost for words. There was no point in arguing that it was Oakhill who'd asset-stripped the business. That he'd earned a legitimate fortune out of Dredge's businesses for years. He felt sick, needed some fresh air.

"I think I'll be leaving now." Dredge stood up and walked out.

Oakhill smirked, picked up his fork and started devouring again. Didn't bother saying goodbye.

Stevie's good humour stayed put for a whole minute. Until a man sat opposite Oakhill at the table. He looked up. Observed the scar, the hard eyes. Recognised one of a kind. A murderer without heart.

Oakhill twisted his head. A second man seated at the neighbouring table. Had a gun discretely trained on his useless, now side-lined bodyguards. He turned back, looked the scarred man in the eyes. Neither blinked.

The waiter appeared, cleared the plates, delivered the next course. Duck. If he noticed Oakhill's companion had changed, he made no sign.

When they were alone again, the scarred man finally spoke. "In case you were wondering, my name is Adam," he said. Oakhill noted the Eastern European accent.

"I know who you are." Didn't add the copper had informed him.

"That is good. Did you appreciate my, ah, little demonstrations?"

"I hadn't really noticed them," Oakhill said. The food went untouched. Both kept their hands on the table surface, in full view.

Adam smiled without pleasure. "Of course. I would have expected no less."

"Let's cut the shit here. What are you after?"

"You. Specifically, your business interests. But that should be no surprise."

Oakhill laughed. "Not a fucking chance."

"I could just take over, but for the sake of world peace, I'm prepared to make you an excellent offer."

"Sure you are." The disbelief was obvious in his tone.

"I will pay you well and let you live. Think of it as a buyout."

"I struggle to accept you will do either of those."

Adam looked genuinely annoyed. A moment later, his face cleared. He smiled. He said, "Believe what you will, but I am a man of honour. I keep my word. I will leave you alone now, but please consider my proposal. I will call you soon to confirm your decision."

Adam stood. Motioned to Ilyas, who rose slowly, keeping his eyes on the bodyguards, gun by his thigh. He left without a backward glance.

Oakhill looked over at his men. Shook his head, furious. "You useless fucking bastards."

Adam had crossed a line, made *direct* contact. Got his phone out, almost crushed the plastic he was so pissed. Made a call to his tame copper. Maybe he could get the Chechens sorted via the almost legit route.

Pressing Buttons

I'm huddling for warmth in the Shit Machine when Dredge exits. I'm tired but, thankfully, the low temperature has kept me awake, because he's out a lot sooner than I expect.

Piles, on the other hand, lying in his racked back seat, looks completely out of it. Dredge stops by the Bentley, swaying in the breeze.

I slip out of my car. No internal light comes on because I've previously removed the bulb (well, it blew, and I couldn't be arsed replacing it, if I'm honest). I leave the door slightly ajar, as it's loud when I slam it, and walk softly up to him.

"Mr Dredge, I'd like a word," I say, attempting official.

He turns to me. Blinks uncertainly, pupils out of focus. Trying to figure if I mean something or not. Or, more precisely, whether I'm someone or not.

"Do you know who I am?" Dredge says. The man is hammered, a slur the width of his car slides through his voice, but he can still string together a sentence that displays his superiority over the less-than-average man that he perceives me to be.

"I addressed you by your name, which gives you a clue that, perhaps, I do."

He laughs. The sound comes from a deep and unwholesome place. "Ah, true. Then what do you want?"

"James Hollowman. Mean anything to you?"

He sobers up fucking quickly then, hammers on the Bentley's window. Piles lifts his head up. Piggy eyes slide from Dredge to me and back again. I deliberately don't meet his gaze, but I see out of my peripheral vision the crease of a frown across his forehead as his little brain realises something is amiss here.

That's my starter for ten.

Dredge says, "No. Should I?" Now his speech really is clear, lucid, direct. He stands more erect, demeanour far more imposing.

"Hollowman was your FD at the now-defunct Dredge Industries. I speak in the past tense, because he was recently found dead in less than salubrious circumstances."

I see lard-arse has popped his door and is trying hard to lever himself out of his seat. He's wheezing like a boiling kettle. If the situation weren't so serious, I'd laugh.

"Oh, him. I remember now. The police are investigating and I'm sure they'll come up with all the answers."

I laugh. "Yeah, right. Let's see, shall we?"

He peers at me then. "Who are you, anyway?"

"What about your COO who disappeared in mysterious circumstances?"

"I have nothing more to say." He waves dismissively, gets in the Bentley, shuts the door, stares ahead as if I don't exist.

However, Piles has finally managed to defeat the challenge of his car seat. Glares at me over the roof. He moves towards me, smile on his flabby face.

"Piles!" Dredge shouts, muffled.

The fat man ignores him, shuffles forward a few more steps. I move as well. I'm fucking angry and up for a fight.

Dredge's window slides down. He shouts again, "Piles, leave him, man!"

He hesitates, glares at me, then returns to his car seat. Leans out, grabs the door, slams it. The locks drop and the engine purrs into life. Piles revs up, the exhaust emitting a throaty roar. He gives me the finger before driving off. At the end of the road, the brake lights flare briefly before the Bentley turns left and disappears.

I let out my angst in a heavy sigh. The bastard hadn't remembered me.

"I'll be seeing you again," I mutter.

The Dildo

"I didn't think you'd be interested in helping me," Emily said.

"You once aided our mutual friend," Mr Lamb replied. "I want to return the favour. And you asked nicely."

They sat in Emily's office, a utilitarian affair in a small building on a non-descript industrial estate. There wasn't even a sign outside to inform anyone this was where her company was located. If you had to ask, you weren't supposed to know.

"How have you been since James was discovered?"

Emily grimaced, aged a decade in a second. "You know, that's all people ever want to talk about. How am I feeling, etc. etc."

"Is there anything wrong with that?"

Emily snorted and ran a manicured hand through blonde hair. "They don't give a shit about me. They're just after gossip. My *feelings* are the least of their concern."

She looked up, perhaps remembering Mr Lamb was here in an unofficial capacity. She opened her mouth to apologise.

Mr Lamb held up a hand. "There's really no need," he said. "I'm not a particularly emotional man anyway."

"Nevertheless, I'm sorry. That was uncalled for. It's just I've been under a lot of stress recently. And some of the performers are playing up today as well. At least the funeral is over now. Perhaps people will let me get on with my life again."

"I'll keep it as brief as possible."

"Thanks."

"Can you tell me when you last saw James?"

"Christ, ages ago! We didn't really see much of each other when we were together, never mind once we'd separated."

"What caused the rift?"

"Him fucking men rather than me." It interested Mr Lamb that she appraised him coolly, watched his reaction. Mr Lamb remained impassive.

"Don't you want to take notes?" Emily asked, noticing Mr Lamb kept his hands folded in his lap.

He tapped his temple with a finger. "Adequate memory."

"Lucky you."

"It's a question of genetics, rather than something as random and unquantifiable as luck."

"Right …"

"When did you speak for the final time?"

She thought for a moment, eyes raised up to the ceiling as she accessed the portion of her brain that stored memories. "A few days before he died, I guess. He called me, out of the blue. It was quite a surprise."

"Did he sound his normal self?"

"Funnily enough, no."

"How was he different?"

"Well, he sounded ... happy. Relieved even."

"And that was irregular?"

"Extremely. James was a workaholic and everything was a worry in case it affected his career."

"Do you know where he was employed?"

"Some legal firm in London. At the time, I didn't have a clue. He started there after we split up. I was so sick of him talking about work when we were married, I took a deliberate approach of determining precisely nothing about his position."

"What about Dredge Industries?"

"I've no idea who they are."

"Why do you think he was happy?"

"Oddly, that's the one thing that's bothered me about this whole affair. I've absolutely no idea."

The door burst open and a large-breasted, partially leather-clad female entered. She was brandishing a huge, double-ended dildo in a clenched fist.

"Emily, we need your help. It's all about to kick the fuck off," she said.

"Give me a moment," Emily replied. "I'm in the middle of a meeting, as you can see."

"Well, don't say you weren't warned. If you hear a scream *in a moment*, it's me battering the heroine to death with this." The girl waved the massive appendage in a manner that was surprisingly threatening for something that quivered so much. The door slammed behind her.

"I'll see myself out," offered Mr Lamb, rising. "I think I've got everything I need for now. Do you mind if I call you, should the need arise?"

"Of course not." She came around the desk and took his hand and held onto it for a moment longer than was necessary, then said, "I'd appreciate it if you would do me one favour."

"If I can."

"When you know what happened to James, please tell me."

"I'll do my best."

"You seem to me you're a man that does significantly better than mere best."

"Thank you."

Then a muffled bawling erupted, which was sharply cut off by a rubbery sounding thud.

"I think I'd better go now," Emily said.

"Well, a fat lot of good you were," Dredge said from the rear seat of the Bentley. The window separating driver from passenger was down. 'Dirty' Harry Piles couldn't help but tense up. He was a little boy again, being told off by his bully of a father.

"You're a fucking useless tub of lard," Dredge continued. "Why do I employ you?"

"It isn't you who pays me," Piles shot back.

He ignored the sideways references to his weight issue. Speed was not an affliction Piles suffered in any aspect of his life. In particular, bowel movements. The trouble with Piles was he suffered a mental problem – a shortage of competent brain cells. That he'd once been a police officer was a constant source of amazement to colleagues and enemies.

"The guy's name is David Brodie," Dredge said. "An old 'friend' of mine we could do without."

Piles lifted his phone up over his shoulder, the screen towards Dredge. He leaned forward and snatched the device. A moment later, Dredge issued a grunt. It may have been an acknowledgement of a job well done, may have been a laugh. Dirty Harry couldn't tell.

"Looks like you've saved yourself for the moment, Piles," Dredge said.

The window whirred up, cutting one world from another. The rest of the journey was in silence.

Back at the house, Dredge sat behind his desk waiting for the call, whiskey in hand. Piles had rung Frank as soon as they returned, told him what had happened, given him the licence plate details. Reporters they could do without.

The telephone jangled. It was an antique thing. Looked good, sound was crap. Dirty Harry snatched at it.

Frank said, "Have you spoken to Stevie?"

"No, boss."

"Good. Keep it that way. Got a pen?"

Piles nodded.

"Did you just nod, Harry?"

"Yeah."

"For fuck's sake. Here's where he'll be. A couple of the boys will come and pick you up. If he moves, I'll give you a call. Got it?"

"Yeah."

Piles replaced the receiver, told Dredge. For the first time that day, Gordon smiled.

Lucy got ready for her date. Is that what it was? She wasn't sure. Meeting someone new was, at least, true. Clothes flew out of the wardrobe as she hunted for the right thing to wear.

First things first. Underwear.

Decent stuff, in case she had to use her charms. Trouble was, nothing matched. And a bra was pointless as she hadn't anything worthy of support. So she went with a cami top.

Then, skirt, dress or trousers? Tights or bare legs? So many decisions.

A couple of outfits later, she thought she had it. Gone for the more casual look. Laid it out, jeans and a blouse, on the bed.

Before dressing, she needed to deal with the peripheral stuff. Tan.

She had to have some colour, even though it was December, because all the men liked it. She'd bought a bottle ages ago, had probably gone off by now. Confirmed it had.

Once applied, she stood in the middle of her room in a scarecrow pose, waiting for the application to dry. She checked her watch. She was going to be fashionably late, shit!

When Lucy thought the bronze was just about right, she flung her clothes on, applied makeup, grabbed the first pair of boots she came across and negotiated the stairs.

"Just going out, Mum!" she shouted.

No reply. Corrie was blaring on the TV. Rough northern accents, the clink of glasses, grating laughter.

Outside, Lucy went to put her footwear on, too late realising she'd picked some ridiculous efforts with huge heels never worn before. No good, they'd have to stay off, because time was pressing. Clutching her shoes in one hand, mini purse in the other, she ran.

Look Out, She's A Ginger

It's an hour since the call from Lucy and I'm full-on regretting my decision. The Shit Machine is outside the place where I lay my hat, although it's all alone because I'm here in the pub, nursing a beer. It's dark and alcoholic, just how I like my women.

I'm currently alone, sitting in a corner, back against the wall. I shouldn't be, but this Lucy bird is late.

It's pretty quiet, which doesn't suit me at all, and the bar staff are lazy bastards. Two drained pint glasses and a consumed packet of nuts gather moss adjacent to my elbow. The door opens and a girl enters.

I don't think I've ever seen anything like her. So tall and slim she looks like an exclamation mark, accentuated by totally unnecessary high heels. She walks like Bambi, legs everywhere. She takes off her woolly hat to reveal a shock of bright ginger in one of those 'I'm stuck with it, so flaunt it' statements. Long, patently false, eyelashes bat over large, wide eyes and her skin is an odd shade of brown as though she's been dipped in lumpy gravy.

Spray tan? Looks more like tar tan.

She hobbles over, almost going over on one ankle.

"Fuck," she mutters.

I look around. Left, right. Yes it's me she's approaching. Oh no, please don't let this be her.

It is.

She pulls out a chair, fingernails scraping down on a blackboard. I cringe and I suspect it won't be the last time tonight.

"You're David, right?" she says in a softened version of the local accent. Like she's lived away for a time, but is rediscovering her roots. She sits, then leans down and pulls a shoe off, deposits it on the table. The heels must be six inches.

"No."

She smiles, puts the second shoe with the first. Pulls out her phone, presses a key with a finger that looks like it belongs on a man's hand. A moment later, my phone rings, jogging on the table surface. She turns her phone to me. It reads, 'David Brodie.'

"Busted," I say.

"Then mine's a vodka," she tells me. "And you're paying because it's my birthday."

"So it is."

After about half an hour, I decide she's all right. A total loser, but that's okay because I am too.

"So you're a journalist?" Lucy asks. She's resting her head on a hand, her arm crooked so she observes me at an angle. As though she sees the world differently to everyone else.

"Not really," I say.

"Well, either you are or you aren't."

"I'm on a story." Bugger, I didn't mean to say that. Must be the alcohol. And I've forgotten how to deal with the opposite sex.

"Sounds fun."

"Trust me, it isn't. Gray said you had something on Dredge."

"No, not really."

"Oh."

"I just told him that so he'd help me. He can't resist a challenge."

"It worked."

She smiled. "And quite well."

The pub door opens again. Hard.

Three guys enter in turn. One is huge. Like asteroid sized. Mostly fat. Probably intimidates people so much they shit their pants without ever needing to raise a fist. I recognise him as Dredge's bodyguard driver, can't remember his name, but his two mates are new to me. They're relatively innocuous for skinhead, card-carrying National Front members. Only a couple of tattoos on their faces.

"I may have a bit of bother coming my way," I say. Not a surprise, because trouble is my shadow.

The fat fucker looks at each person in the pub. He takes his time. The skinheads simply exude aggression, daring anyone to take them on. Fatty finally sees me. Recognition strides across his face and his legs kick into motion. The skinheads trail in his monstrous wake.

He stops at my table. Smiles down at me. "Hello again."

His voice sounds as if it emanates from a cave. His breath smells like it too, musty and dank. There's no was this guy is getting the girls unless he pays for it.

I say nothing.

Fatty turns his gaze to Lucy. "You probably want to fuck off, love, unless you like a smack, that is."

I shit you not but the skinheads giggle like a pair of girls.

"I'll remain where I am, thanks."

"Have it your own way."

I stand up, circumnavigate the table and situate myself between the trio and Lucy. I've no idea what's wrong with me, because chivalry is an attitude I don't think I've ever displayed.

"You need to stay away," Fatty Fuckwit Piles says to me, prods me in the chest.

"No idea what you're talking about," I reply.

"He said you'd say that." Fatty smirks at the skinheads. They attempt to intensify their glare and keep their laser beam eyes fixed on me, not Sir Wankalot.

"Who did? Dredge?"

He snorts. I assume it's a laugh.

"I'm going to punch you so hard," he says with a smirk in his voice, "your features are going to end up on the wall over there." He points.

I know what's coming next because I've been here before. Not *here* exactly. I mean this situation, where big fuckers want to execute unpleasant activities on my face and I'm not prepared to quietly accept a mauling. Plus I've no regard for my health.

The key is to start first. Three to one. Not bad odds.

Piles is the least of my issues. He's a big guy and, once he's down, he's not getting back up in a year of Sundays. He'll roll around like a whale in a mud-wrestling competition.

It's the other two. All depends on how tough they actually are versus their assumption.

I turn my eyes to where my face is supposed to 'end up'. I don't need to be looking at someone to connect my extremities to theirs.

"Look, lads, can we discuss this?" I say, and that's when I kick Fatty McBastard in the nuts.

He emits a deep groan, sags and leans on one of the skinheads for support, but an RSJ would bend under his load.

I step forward and head-butt his mate before comprehension is ready to trigger a response. I feel the crunch of his nose on my forehead, the splash of something hot and tacky – there's no way it's my blood. A rabbit punch to his solar plexus and he's down with the wallowing Fatty, who's pinned the other skinhead firmly to the deck. He's flapping like a butterfly until I hit him hard on the jaw. Out cold.

"You'll regret this," Fatty yells at me.

"Yeah, yeah," I reply as I walk away.

"Somebody, help me up," I hear him shout.

"That was good," Lucy says, shoes in hand.

"Fancy a drink at my place?

She nods. I smile.

We negotiate our way through the silent pub, end up outside in the freezing air.

Despite my apparent good humour, there's one thing that bothers me. How did they get onto me so quickly. And why?

Okay, that's two things. But still, all the same ...

Clearing Up

The copper entered the cul-de-sac. It was still relatively early, 10.30pm or so, but there were no lights on in the abodes. All the residents had to be diligent employees of a faceless corporation. Abed at a decent time, scared to be late for work in case some heartless bastard fired them. The copper shrugged. Not his problem. Felt nothing but disdain for the spineless civilians.

The copper walked up to a shabby looking detached house. Checked address with memory. It was correct. The front garden looked like it hadn't been tended for a while. Gate lying on the lawn, grass growing through it. Weeds on the drive. Tried the front door. Locked. Sensible.

Went round the back. Locked, too. The copper raised a foot, kicked out hard. It gave. Another boot and the jamb was in pieces, lock broken off. Waited a moment. Didn't hear an alarm or anyone coming to investigate.

The copper lurched the splintered wood out of the way and entered the kitchen – literally bare. Through into the hallway. Flicked a switch. A low wattage bulb emitted dim light. Depressing little place. Stained carpet, plain walls, no furniture to speak of.

Then went upstairs and started to search. Nothing to trash, very few hiding places. A mattress in one of the three bedrooms was the only item not bolted down. Zero underneath it.

Back down to the ground floor. Living room was just a chair, which got kicked over, and a bag for life from a well-known food store. The copper picked it up, glanced inside, smiled grimly. Walked back out to the car. Most people would think it a heap of shit, but the copper knew it was a classic. Sighed. Such a pity. Nevertheless, put a rusty lump of metal through the windscreen which generated a satisfying shatter.

By the time lights started to flick on, the copper had done in all the windows on the old banger and was about to take out the headlamps.

Decided to leave it there. Looked enough like a mindless robbery. The copper departed. A good night's work.

Unwelcome Visitors

We're walking along the road back home. Even though Lucy doesn't have her shoes on, she's my height. Which makes her lofty, because I'm a good six feet. I've my hands in my pockets. It's fucking freezing. She slips her arm through the crook of mine and huddles closer for warmth. Walking barefoot surely can't help.

She might be tall, but she's not in the same league as me when it comes to looks. I'm way ahead. I don't like to brag (but I will). I was rather cool when I was younger. The birds loved me. Girlfriends had to change their knickers three or four times a day, at least, just being with me. I sighed. Wished it was actually true, rather than something I just told myself. How could it be so long ago so quickly?

My back's beginning to throb from hunching my shoulders by the time we arrive at my house. You know when you try and keep yourself warmer by making yourself smaller? It doesn't work.

I slow as we enter the street. Something's not right.

I don't need to rely on a sixth sense, because the fact is right in front of my face. The windscreen of the Shit Machine has been smashed in. And I don't mean a small hole. It's been taken out completely. In fact, all the windows have been busted to bollocks. There's glass everywhere. It's like a tornado has touched down in the street, but only landed on my car.

"Somebody's unlucky night," says Lucy.

"Mine," I reply, peering inside.

There're shards everywhere. I'm not concerned if anything's been nicked, because I've nothing of value. The sound system consists of medium wave radio and a cassette player.

"Oh well, the insurance will cover it," Lucy says. She sees my face bathed in streetlight yellow, makes a statement, "You don't have any, do you?"

I shake my head. "Or a licence. Or tax."

"It'll be some kids, I bet."

I shake my head again. "Too thorough. Someone took their time over this."

I unlock the boot, look inside. Laptop and cash are still there, thank Christ. Close it again.

"I'm starting to sober up," she says, interrupting my relief. "And it's bloody freezing. Where's that drink you promised me?"

She pulls me towards my abode. My feet drag. I unlock the front door. Illumination weakly spills out. Odd, I didn't think I'd left it on. If the car hadn't been totalled, I'd have assumed negligence with the electricity supply, but now my immediate assumption is someone's been inside.

Put my key in the lock, push at the painted wood with a finger. It doesn't move, because the hinges need oiling. I straight-arm it instead. The crack widens into a few feet of breach. I can peer into the hallway.

Stairs stretch up to the left. The living room entrance is a few feet in front and to the right. The kitchen straight ahead.

All the lights burn, which in itself is wrong. And the boot marks that darken my already skanky carpet. Lucy steps inside. She gets on her knees and takes a closer look at them.

Where Lucy treads, I follow.

"A tall man, I'd guess," she says. "See the distance between the footprints?"

I nod. "I'm impressed."

Lucy shrugs, like it's no biggie.

The kitchen looks okay, at least the kettle is still in one piece, but the back door is busted in. I lift it up, try and slot it back in place. It doesn't work that well. The cold air whistles through the gaps.

"Oh my God!" I hear Lucy shout from the living room.

I enter. My worst firms are confirmed. They've gone to town in there – my chair is upside down. What had it ever done to them?

"Bastards!" I say.

"They've stolen everything!" Lucy says.

I don't disavow her of her error. I feel mildly embarrassed for some reason. I've no need to impress this girl, so I don't know why I say, "Yeah, looks like it."

"Insurance?" she asks.

I shake my head. She rolls her eyes. "Where's the booze? We need to get really pissed!"

"Kitchen."

As she departs on said alcohol pursuit, I turn my chair back over. One of the legs is bent and it leans drunkenly. That's okay. When I'm bombed, it'll seem straight again.

But the supermarket bag is gone, the one with Gowan's stuff in. It's the only item that was here when I left, but isn't on my return.

"It's all right," Lucy shouts from the kitchen. "They haven't had the vodka away."

"Phew!" I say. That stuff goes with everything except decisions.

"Have you got any glasses?" she shouts again.

Relieved, I recall the ones I nicked from the pub this morning. "Yes, try the sink."

Lucy enters, pours a slug into a wet wine glass, hands it to me. Gets one for herself, holds the goblet up for a toast.

We clink. She knocks it back in one go, grimaces.

"Some birthday this is," she says.

"I've had worse."

"Are you okay?"

"Yeah," I say and smile.

But it's short-lived, because there in the doorway is a man.

With a scar, a friend and a gun.

It's A Steal

Konstantin looked up from the sheaf of papers he'd been examining, reading glasses perched on the end of his nose. They were a recent affectation and not one he cared for. Frankly, they were embarrassing. He was seated at a small table in his living room, a laptop and cup of steaming coffee by his side.

"We need talk," he said.

Mr Lamb could hear the question mark in his voice. He looked up from his Sudoku problem, suppressed a sigh. He'd been attempting to beat his record time and, in the process, unwind before retiring to the spare bedroom for no more than three hours recuperation. He put The Times down, interlinked his fingers, and gave his full and very direct attention to Konstantin. Said, "Found something?"

The Russian nodded. "First, data Meadows gave us. Anomalies regarding Dredge's companies."

"Let me guess, Oakhill isn't clean."

"Very murky financials."

Konstantin turned around his laptop to reveal a complex spreadsheet detailing the movement of money, in some cases particularly large sums, across a tangled web of accounts for a company called KnockOut Ventures, located in the Cayman Islands.

He continued, "But gaps in information, what's gone where. Authorities very careful to protect their clients."

Mr Lamb knew that much to be true. No-one chose to locate a business in a place like that unless they wanted secrecy. He said, "There's someone I think can help with this. In the meantime, keep digging. Anything else?"

"This." Konstantin threw a photograph onto the desk. "And this." More photographs, landing haphazardly one on top of the other. Four in all.

Mr Lamb ordinarily didn't do unnecessary gestures, but he was with Konstantin and had to modify his behaviour accordingly. So he shrugged. Said, "And?"

"All dead."

Mr Lamb leaned forward. This was much more interesting than a spreadsheet and mythical financial transactions. Dodgy bankers undertook these day in, day out, as he well knew. He picked up the photos and leafed through.

"All of them?"

"Da."

"Him." Konstantin tugged the bundle away from Mr Lamb and put them back on the table. He selected a colour shot of a man with very ginger hair, pulled it to the top of the pile. "Died in a car accident. Her ..." A blonde, lots of make-up. "... threw herself off a bridge. This one ..." A man, bespectacled and balding. "Hit and run cycling accident."

"Okay, I get the picture." *A black one,* Mister Lamb thought. "Jobs?"

"Varied," Konstantin said. "But all reasonably senior."

"What does Meadows' file have on the investigation?"

Konstantin paused a moment before he said, "Nothing. This my work. Coroner's report say accidents or death by misadventure. No-one else involved."

"Incredibly convenient."

Konstantin nodded. "Or efficient."

They looked at each other momentarily.

"There's another one," Konstantin said and threw a fifth photo on the pile. "Just heard about him."

"Who's he?"

"Nigel Gowan. Very odd. Died two months ago." Konstantin flicked to an archive newspaper article describing the disappearance of Dredge Industries Chief Operating Officer. "But body turn up today."

"So?"

"He only actually dead one day, not sixty."

"Once I've been to see my friend, we need to talk to Dredge," Mr Lamb decided.

Konstantin nodded.

And theatrically smacked fist into palm.

"Got a kicking, did you Harry?" Dredge asked when he saw the marks on Piles's face and thunder on his brow. "Couldn't have happened to a nicer man."

Dredge's nose was Santa Claus red, a direct consequence of the excessively large jigger of brandy he'd part consumed (and the three previously). He swirled the liquid remnants around in a glass that would more accurately have been termed a vase.

"Fuck you," Dirty Harry shot back. He poured a slug for himself, ignoring Dredge's affected, but ultimately powerless, glare.

Piles enjoyed rubbing the old fool's nose in it. A class-based role reversal as the 'servant' got one over the 'master'. It was the arrogance of the wealthy and successful that always led to their downfall.

It amused him that it was the lower echelons, the likes of him, to which they always turned to save their arse. Which reminded him. He pulled out his phone.

"Sure that's wise, Harry, my good pal?"

"What are you on about old man?"

"Think about it. Use that miniscule brain of yours for a moment. Consider how your boss is going to react when you tell him that three thugs badly lost out to one washed up hack."

Harry considered Dredge's advice. Regrettably concluded that he was correct. Another little score for the fucker. Well, one day, soon.

He put his phone away, caught the tiny smirk on Dredge's lips. Harry's temper flared again. He picked up the crystal decanter, topped up his glass to its rim. Then he held the expensive cut glass vessel at arm's length in front of him. The significantly costlier amber liquid within glimmered.

Harry smiled at a pale Dredge, released his grip. A second later a huge crash, glass and brandy splattered everywhere.

"You'll need to clear that up, Gordon," Harry said. "Pity you don't have the maids to do that anymore for you."

Where's Eve?

So, there's some guy standing in the entrance to the living room. I've never seen him before. Hard eyes, blonde hair, scar across his cheek.

"I saw your door was open," he said. Good English, accented. He threw a thumb over his shoulder. "My friend Ilyas here doesn't speak your language. So no sudden movements in case he shoots you. Understand?"

I nod.

He says, "Good. In my country, it is customary for a host to offer his friend a drink."

"Well, we're not in your country, and we're certainly not friends," Lucy says. My heart stops.

The scarred man surprisingly barks out a laugh. "She is feisty! My name is Adam. I know you are David Brodie, but you," he points at Lucy, "I not know."

"And it's staying that way," she says. The smile drops off Adam's face. So does the temperature in the room. Suddenly, the atmosphere is as icy as a penguin's testicles.

"It's vodka," I say to ease the tension. He turns to look at me. The scar is red, angry. A question mark in his eye for a moment, until he figures out what I'm talking about.

"Russian?" Adam spat the word, like it left a dirty taste in his mouth.

"No, Polish."

"Hmm, a slight improvement, but I will still pass, I think. Best to keep a clear head. Believe it or not, it's harder to suitably hurt people when drunk. You need clarity to really inflict pain."

I dry gulp. All the moisture in my mouth has evaporated. I take a swallow of the vodka. It soaks into my tongue like a bucket of water onto baked sand. Gone in moments.

"What do you want?" Lucy asks.

Adam swings his gaze onto her. He smiles. The scar is back to a more normal, dead white colour.

"I want to give you something, not to take anything," he says.

I'm confused and make that clear.

"I've a message. Stay away from Steven Oakhill. Keep your nose out of business that doesn't concern you."

"I've never even heard of him," I say.

Which is true. An hour ago, a warning to stay away from Dredge. Now this guy. What the fuck is going on?

Adam clearly thinks I'm wittingly playing his game and grins again. I wish he'd stop doing that. It's downright scary.

He says, "Good. You are a cleverer man than I had been led to believe."

"Thanks." I don't mean it.

"I will leave you two lovebirds in peace now. Do not worry, I have no intention of harming you, as this is just a friendly chat. But …" He stares at me hard. "If I am forced to return, I will not be a happy man. Come, Ilyas."

He and his trigger-happy mate leave. So does the strength from my body. I collapse into my chair. Lucy, though, goes to the window, looks out (no curtains to twitch) and watches them drive away. When she turns around, she has a thoughtful expression on her face, but then it slides into a wink.

"Another drink?" she says.

I nod.

Then I remember.

Lovebirds?!

Ups And Downs

The copper entered his temporary place of rest. A rather plush penthouse flat with a sea view. Opened the window, listened to the crash of the waves, ignored the stiff freezing wind that blew in through the gap. The copper sniffed the air, detected the salt.

It was a good place to hide, no garden to maintain and a Hungarian cleaner to tidy up afterwards. The perfect domestic life.

Sat down with a can of Stella and a spliff. Took a heavy hit of the latter, held the smoke within lungs for as long as possible, then blew it out in an impressive stream. Finished both can and toke before turning to the paperwork lifted from Brodie's place.

Documentation poured onto a coffee table, the copper sifted through it. Didn't understand most of it. Loads of numbers in columns on sheet after curling sheet, a folder full of e-mails between Gowan and Dredge, scrawled hand-written notes, dates and times.

They appeared to be a testimony of events Gowan had recorded. Of course, the copper knew all about witness statements. Had falsified enough.

Oakhill's name popped up in the middle of one of the notes. The copper went back to the beginning and read through. It took a few minutes to cover the same ground, but more slowly this time. Decided there was nothing dangerous within.

Another spliff. The copper stood by the window and smoked it down to the roach to celebrate. Saluted Gowan's soul and wondered where his corpse was now.

Gordon Dredge was slumped in his study, remaining brandy in one hand, cigar in the other. Stocks were running low on both items. His expenditure was strictly controlled these days. It was like having the receiver in.

Luxury items were deemed off limits, too costly. But Dredge had made sure there was some 'contraband' smuggled away before the restrictions were imposed. His was an old house, lots of nooks and crannies. There were probably plenty even he hadn't yet discovered.

Dredge swirled the liquid in the glass, watched how it glinted through the crystal diamonds. He did his best thinking whilst drunk, on his own in his study. At the pinnacle of his achievements, Dredge had been a formidable businessman.

Lauded, respected, feared.

But it was those two little words – *had been*.

How time caught up with everyone, erased you, levelled you. No matter how strong you think you are, you're nothing compared to the relentless march of time.

Everyone gets old.

Dredge shivered. He felt a finger of fear caress his spine. Fear of his imminent mortality. Then … anger. With himself more than anyone.

He wasn't gone yet, but here he was imagining himself in the ground. He was his own ghost of Christmas Future.

He had two choices:

Do nothing.
Do something.

Let Oakhill do as he wished.
Or fight him.

Before he was turfed out onto the street. He might only have a matter of days, but he'd use it.

One thing Dredge was – a fighter. And a dirty one at that.

This Brodie fellow. He seemed to have caused a reaction. Gordon wondered if he could somehow exploit that …

He swirled the brandy and thought it through, long into the night.

The Dead Man's ... Dead

Three Days Ago

I wake up. Wonder if it's been a dream. Feel a body next to me.

After the departure of Adam and his silent killer friend, we'd drunk vodka from the stolen wine glasses until the wee small hours, shared a fag, retreated upstairs. I'd offered to sleep in the chair, but Lucy wouldn't hear of it.

Lucy is in the bed, if a mattress can be described so. Nothing happened, I assure you. We're fully clothed.

It's nice and warm in here. I'm reluctant to get out from under the covers and into what will be an ice box. So I lie on my back, watching the grey clouds scud across the sky and consider my extremely limited progress to date.

An odd meeting with a dead man, who I can't contact anymore.

I've been robbed, but I've no idea who stole the file. I conclude it has to be Dredge's boys. Perhaps the fat bastard in the pub was a diversion while they caned my car and the house? Perhaps not. It doesn't do to jump to conclusions, I've learned.

But there are a couple of positives.

First, I still have the money, hidden in the Shit Machine's boot. I'm the wealthiest I've been for some time.

Second, I might not have the documents, but I still have the data on the USB stick which is in my trousers. And now I know someone wants it.

I'll take this opportunity to confess ... I hadn't actually read everything before I went to see Dredge. I simply figured it would be a laugh to wind him up.

That was a fuck-up, clearly.

There's a third positive.

I don't have a hangover. Drinking regularly seems to generate resilience in me. Or perhaps the headache never gets the chance to catch up with the alcohol expulsion. Whichever it is, I cover all the bases and keep myself nicely topped up.

Someday, I'll have the headache from Hell. But I'll probably be dead by then anyway.

I look at Lucy, in the daylight this time – all men know that the opposite sex appear literally the opposite of how they had the night before.

One of her incredibly long legs protrudes from the duvet. It seems to stretch out forever, like a runway. A false lash is hanging off her left eyelid. Some lipstick is smeared across her frowning face. Her hair is mussed and there's a streak of white on her cheek, where some of the tan has rubbed off onto the pillow. She's no chest to speak of, which is a major disadvantage, but overall she doesn't seem a bad girl in looks or personality.

That she's still here, having spent an evening with me, is a major achievement.

I'm sorely tempted to go back to sleep, but I tell myself I'm a better man than that (I'm not, trust me), that I've things to do if I'm going to solve the mystery.

With a suppressed groan of lethargy, I slowly slide off the mattress. Lucy doesn't wake. I'm pleased to see I took my shoes off, but not so pleased when I trip over one of them. A glance over my shoulder reassures me she's still unconscious, despite my racket.

The stairs creak as I descend. In the kitchen, I make a proper coffee. Once suitably brewed, I sit down in my leaning chair, pat the arm lovingly. I still can't believe the bastards turned it over. If I get them for anything, it'll be that.

I sit there for half an hour, my coffee steadily cooling, whilst I think about the Dredge case.

Don't get very far.

"Morning," Lucy says from the doorway.

"There's coffee in the kitchen," I say, with what I hope is a contemplative expression attached to my features.

"You constipated?" Lucy asks.

I wonder whether to share my information with her. I open my mouth to speak, but she beats me to it.

"The Police are coming, by the way."

I look up and out the window. She's right. What do they want?

The two cops introduce themselves as DCI Troon – tall, grey, and smartly dressed, and DS Gregory – bordering on middle-aged, slightly overweight, and with an attitude.

"Brodie and Ryan," I reply.

Sounds like a comedy duo. Don't feel like laughing, though.

Gregory looks around the room, a barely disguised sneer on his cheese-grater face that soaks through into his voice. "Had some *trouble*, sir?"

"No," I lie. Smile disarmingly, stick two fingers up mentally.

"So the smashed-up vehicle and emptied house are *normal*?"

"Pretty much. I'm not materialistic, and the car is my fault. I was incredibly drunk."

"Right, sir." Gregory gives Troon a disbelieving look.

His boss remains utterly impassive. Says in a low Scottish burr, "We'd like to speak with you, Mr Brodie."

"Enunciate away."

"A body was discovered late evening yesterday."

"And what does that have to do with me?"

"You're probably the last person he was with."

"I don't understand." I say this because it's true. Had one of the skinheads got it in the neck?

"Out on Sandwich Bay."

My stomach knots up, although my face doesn't. I shrug, say, "Perhaps you'd better explain your point."

Gregory steps in. "The body, when identified, was of a man who was believed to have died several months ago. One Nigel Gowan."

"All sounds very bizarre."

"We also understand you met with this man."

"And what gives you that impression?"

"Witnesses inform us you were at the golf clubhouse."

"So were a number of others. I parked next to their cars."

"So you admit to being there?"

"I've never denied it."

"And do you *deny* asking for Mr Gowan?"

"No. But so what?"

Gregory opens his mouth to speak, but Troon interrupts. "And then what did you do?" Sharp eyes analyse me, unamused mouth opens again. "And before you twist the truth for a second time. we know you didn't leave immediately."

"Look, am I under arrest here?"

"Would you prefer we take you to the station. Mr Brodie?"

"No, of course not."

"Then consider yourself a good citizen helping us with our enquiries. unless otherwise notified."

I hold Troon's gaze for a moment. He stares back unblinking, a hint of a challenge in his eyes.

I sigh. "I went for a walk on the beach. I've never been out that way before."

"Did you meet anybody?" Gregory again.

"The place was deserted. Just seagulls and golfers for company."

Troon is obviously unconvinced, but there's fuck all he can do.

I know it. He knows it. I try hard not to smile.

"Is something *funny*. sir?" Gregory asks.

Oops, busted. "No, I'm just in a delightful mood today. Anything else I can help you with, officers?"

"That'll be all for now, sir. But if you do think of something ..." Gregory hands a business card over with his mobile phone number and e-mail address on.

Yeah right, like that's going to happen.

I turn to Troon, say, "Do you have a card for me?"

"They're at the printers," he replies.

"Can you see yourselves out?"

"My pleasure," Gregory says. "I wouldn't want *your* sort escorting me."

The front door shuts none too gently. I watch them walk down my path. Troon seems to give Gregory a brief ear bashing. I can see the younger man's cheeks redden from here. Then they get into an unmarked car and sod off.

Lucy lets out a huge sigh, says, "What did he mean when he said 'your sort'?"

"Nothing major. Had a run in with the cops last year. It was all bullshit," I mumble.

My mind is elsewhere. Specifically Sandwich.

Gowan's dead. Again. The question is, who killed him this time?

And why?

Blast From The Past

Mr Lamb waited. For a prison, the room was relatively comfortable.

Yes, there was only a single table with two accompanying hard chairs. Yes, the room was secured. However, the atmosphere of fear that pervaded your average lock-up was absent. There was even reasonable piece of carpet covering the floor.

A key rattled in the lock, the door swung back on its hinges, and the prisoner shuffled in. His shoulders were hunched, hair a mess, skin sallow. Incarceration had not been kind on Ian Culpepper.

Mr Lamb nodded at the guard, who backed out. From the look on his face, the man clearly didn't like it. But orders were orders. And they came straight from the warden.

The lock mechanism clanked again and they were alone. Culpepper loitered by the table, head down, unmoving. Like he was waiting for an order.

"Why don't you sit, Ian?" Mr Lamb pulled the chair out for him and the ex-bank Chairman lowered himself slowly down, clasping his arms across his chest as if he was cold or protecting himself. "How are you?"

No response.

Mr Lamb placed himself opposite. Between them lay a sheaf of papers crammed with numbers in a fine text – a printout of Meadows' data. He pushed them under Culpepper's nose. Then sat back, waited. He had all day. So did Culpepper. And another four years on top of that. The man had lost everything. He was bankrupt, unemployed and divorced. His imminent knighthood shelved. Permanently.

But most of all, he'd lost his status – the one thing Culpepper had fought to preserve – when he'd been convicted of fraud. The murder charge hadn't stuck, despite the prosecution's best efforts. Once sentenced, Culpepper's last few remaining friends pulled some strings and had him placed in an open prison to see out his term.

It was more than ten minutes before Culpepper twitched a muscle. His leg jerked. Then again. Began a repetitive jiggle. Culpepper pressed his hands down on his thigh, looked up at Mr Lamb.

"Why are you here?" he asked. His voice sounded scrawny, stripped of its customary muscular timbre.

"To see if you're willing to redeem yourself."

"Coming from you, that is an incredible statement."

"I've never pretended to anything other than what I am."

"I don't accept that."

Mr Lamb returned Culpepper's stare. "I may be able to get your sentence reduced," he said.

Silence for a minute, eyeballs locked.

"What must I do in return? In here, everything is a trade."

"I'd have thought that would be second nature to you, Ian."

"That's a cheap shot."

Mr Lamb allowed the insult to brush past him. Said, "There are some financial statements in front of you. I'd appreciate your opinion."

"Is that all?"

"For now."

Culpepper's eyes flicked down. Tipped his head onto his shoulder. Mr Lamb observed the man's leg had stopped shaking. Culpepper put out a hand. Pulled it back again as if he'd received a static shock. Slowly extended the limb again. Fingers manoeuvred the documentation closer, grasped them.

He stood and read as he walked. Flicked through the pages, back and forth across the small room. Mr Lamb was fascinated by the transformation. The ex-Chairman straightened up, and shifted back in time to the man of considerable power and influence that he once was. It was like watching an actor on stage fall into his part within a couple of strides. Remarkable.

Culpepper returned to his seat after five minutes of pacing. He leaned forward, elbows on the table. Spun the paper towards Mr Lamb.

"Look at this," he said. Tapped the paper with a claw. Mr Lamb noticed the nail was broken, dirt smeared underneath.

"Fascinating. Multiple transfers across accounts, large quantities prior, smaller post movement."

"The money's being laundered?"

"Well done, Lamb! Whoever these accounts belong to is one wealthy person."

"Could you trace the source?"

"Yes. Given enough time, data and access to external networks, I could tell you exactly what's gone where."

Mr Lamb sat back a moment. Weighed up the risks.

"Okay," he said. "I'll get you a laptop, an internet link and all the information I can."

It was Culpepper's opportunity to sit back. He said, "What's in it for me?"

"I've already told you. We'll look at your sentence."

"I want that in writing."

"Sorry, Ian, I can't do that."

"Why fucking not?"

"In case you don't come through. No guarantees up front."

"Then I'm not doing it."

Mr Lamb stood up, took the dominant position. Stuck out a hand, palm up. Said, "Papers please."

Culpepper looked down at the sheaf. Pulled them to his chest like a child, dropped his eyes to the table.

Mr Lamb could see the thoughts skittering over his face. Once he passed the pile over, any connection to his old life would be gone again. Eventually, he looked up.

"Do I have your word?" Mr Lamb could see Culpepper hated having to even ask.

"For what it's worth, yes."

Culpepper sighed heavily. "Okay, I'll do it."

"Everything will be with you tomorrow at 9am."

"Can I keep these?"

"Of course."

"Thank you. I won't let you down."

Which saddened Mr Lamb more than anything.

As he left, he threw a glance over his shoulder. Saw Culpepper hunched over, shoulders shaking.

Meet The Parent

It's a couple of hours since the cops left. The atmosphere of arrogance has just about cleared from the air.

Lucy's had a shower, sorted her hair out. It hangs in long, coppery strands. Without the tan, she looks as pale as a ghost, except for the speckling of freckles, but a damn sight better for not having all that brown crap on her face. She's growing on me, although she's still too thin. I've seen slices of lean bacon with more fat on them.

"Do you mind if I hang around with you for a few days?" she asks, over a mug of tea.

"Erm ..."

"I'm not proposing I move in or anything. Just while we've got the story going."

Note the 'we' in the above statement. But then I think it's not a bad thing to have her around. She's pretty good company.

So I say, "Aye, fuck it. Why not?"

"Good, because I need to get some clothes first ..."

We're in the small living room at the front of the terraced house in which Lucy resides. Everything here feels shoved together in a space that's slightly too tight. There are four moth-eaten armchairs mobbed with cushions and throws, an ancient TV the size of a coffin, and a fireplace crammed with bric-a-brac.

Photographs smother one wall, a large crucifix hangs on another. But what dominates is a photo in a silver frame that's shrouded in funeral black. It hangs by itself. I'd taken a sneaky peek on arrival. A young man smiling into the lens.

Mrs Lucy enters the room with a tray on which perch three cups and saucers. They're mismatched. She sets the collection down none too gently on a little table.

You know it's said the daughter ends up looking like the mother? Well, in this case, dear mama has wrinkles across her face you could electrify and run a tram along, several murder of crows' feet around her eyes and lips that look like they've been opened with a razor blade – severe and blood red. Her frizzy hair is bleached blonde, the brown roots already showing half an inch. And she's wearing an apron.

"Would you like one lump or two?" Lucy's mother asks, her voice sounding like it's been punched several times.

"None and no milk either," I reply. Then I see her spoon two massive piles of sugar into my tiny cup and a slug of cow juice too. She stirs. If there's any coffee still present, it'll have retreated into a metaphoric corner to lap at its wounds.

As she moves to hand me the cup, Mrs Lucy somehow manages to knock the little table, which wobbles precariously. It's a result, because most of my sugary milk slops into the saucer and onto the tray. I try hard to suppress the sigh of relief.

"Ah, feck it," she says, stands, retreats out to the kitchen.

"I told you she was weird," Lucy whispers.

Yeah, about five minutes ago as she put her key in the lock. Since then, I've been bombarded by oddity.

"What the fuck are we doing here?" I rasp, although I reckon I could shout at the top of my lungs and Mrs Lucy wouldn't register.

"I haven't been home for a day, I wanted to make sure she was all right."

"So this is a flying visit?"

She nods. Smiles at me a little sheepishly.

Mrs Lucy returns then with a dishcloth. Picks up my cup, pours the liquid from the saucer into it. Half full now. She then mops up the dregs in the tray, squeezes the rag, topping said cup up to the rim. Mrs Lucy hands me the dregs. Her daughter feigns disinterest, but I can see she's trying extremely hard not to laugh. She's seen it all before, I'll bet.

I peer inside.

There's all sorts of crap floating around on top, including an oily scum that's more than likely washing up liquid.

I figure I've had worse. But not very often.

Mrs Lucy sags back into her chair. "So, you're the new wee fella?" she peppers me with a shotgun blast of Northern Irish brogue. Belfast maybe?

"Mam!" Lucy scolds.

"I'm only enquiring over my solitary offspring! I can't lose another, now can I?"

Lucy looks downcast at this. My silently held suspicion that the mortuary picture on the mantelpiece is of her brother now looks to be a racing certainty.

I see nicotine-stained fingers shake a little with suppressed emotion as Mrs Lucy stuffs a fag in her mouth and sparks up. Half the cancer stick is gone in a single inhale. I'm not offered one, so I suck in as much second-hand smoke as I can.

Two drags and she's stubbing it out, I hope into an ashtray, but she's leant over in her chair and it hides whatever the container is from me. She sits back up, smoothes her apron out. The cigarette seems to have helped her calm down a bit.

I'm totally wrong. It gives her a second, gale force wind.

"Lucy," she says, "Would you mind clearing the things away and let me have a word with your wee fella?"

"He's not my wee …"

"Clear away. Now."

"Yes, mam."

"And shut the feckin' door behind you."

I open my mouth, but don't get a chance to speak. She raises a finger at me that looks as if it's been ground into a point by a pencil sharpener. My jaws clamp shut.

Once Lucy has retreated, her mother leans over and grins. Well, sort of exposes her teeth as she peels her lips back. Looks like an amused chimpanzee. Is she going to take a bite out of me? I hope not, I'll catch something for sure if she does. I know I wish for a hastened death, but there're some things I'll draw the line at.

"What do you intend with our Lucy?" she asks, peering at me.

"Intend?"

"Don't play the feckin' eejit with me! Answer the feckin' question!"

"I don't *intend* anything with Lucy, Mrs Ryan."

"But she was with you last night. Is my Lucy just a cheap shag to you?"

"We barely know each other Mrs ..."

"I'm well aware, from bitter experience, what you men are like," she cuts in.

I go for non-committal. "Okay."

"I had a man once."

"That many?" I cringe, expecting a reaction.

She doesn't. Probably didn't hear me. Her eyes have gone all dreamy and distant. It's either recollection or wind.

"Three children I've had. All born the way God intended and feckin' painful I can tell you. I screamed like I had the Devil himself inside me, trying to pop out."

Sounds weird? It gets worse.

She says, "No matter how proud of it you think you are, I'll have you know there's no chance of you having anything in there ..." She aims the pointy digit at my crotch. "... that'd be bigger going into my vagina than what came out."

I have to say I'm completely lost for words. I'm not sure whether she's propositioning me, threatening me, or just plain lost it.

"You'll have to look after our Lucy. My other daughter is in Australia with her husband. My son, God rest him, is in a better place. My vagina's broken, so I'll not be having any more kids. So there's just my Lucy. She's had more than her fair share of troubles and doesn't need you adding to them."

Lucy, thank fuck, chooses to come back in right then, large holdall in hand. The living room door dislodges the heavy atmosphere as though its smoke being wafted away.

"Are you guys getting on?" she asks.

"Like a feckin' fire on house," Mrs Ryan says. "Aren't we son?" She leans over, pats my leg. Sparks up again, takes a long drag. "Now will you two eejits fuck off? I've the TV to watch and you're cramping my style."

I'm gratefully opening the front door when Mrs Ryan calls Lucy back.

"Hang on a moment," she says, rolling her eyes.

I move nearer the sitting room. Out of concern for Lucy, of course. No prying intended on my part.

"Is that who you're running with now?" asks Mrs Ryan in a hoarse whisper.

"Maybe," Lucy says, non-commital, but a little smile in her voice.

I grimace.

"Well, fair fucks to you, love. And with that shitty hair style you have on you, who'd have thought it? Now clear off."

I sidle to the front door again so Lucy doesn't suspect I've heard any of the exchange.

"You okay?" Lucy asks.

I nod so not to betray the lie. It's not good if Lucy is beginning to feel an attachment. People get hurt around me. I think I'll have to do something about that before too long.

Watching Brief

"I hate stakeouts," Konstantin growled.

"You should be used to standing around," Mr Lamb said without sarcasm. A blank stare from the Russian was lost on him.

"Da. Had purpose then. But this? *Dull.*" He yawned again.

"For God's sake, Konstantin," Mr Lamb said, the merest hint of frustration creeping into his tone.

"I just bored," the Russian said with a dismissive wave. "No action."

The pair were scrutinising Dredge's house through powerful ocular instruments – a broad telescope and a camera with the kind of zoom lens a sports photographer would envy.

They'd managed to access the nearest neighbour's house. The owner was away and, they understood, would be for several days yet. Plenty of time to achieve what they needed.

The plan was a simple one. Should Dredge and Piles make a move, Konstantin would follow. Mr Lamb would remain behind to undertake some internal reconnaissance.

So far, the surveillance had been entirely uneventful, but it was only a matter of hours old:

No visitors.

Dredge had been barely in evidence.

The bodyguard, Piles, looked as bored as Konstantin. Appeared regularly at the front door for a smoke.

Here he was again.

Mr Lamb switched to the camera, took a shot of Piles as he walked out of the house. Arm extended, he pointed towards the car. The Bentley's boot lid popped. Dirty Harry put something inside, slammed it closed, leant against the bodywork, sparked up a cigarette.

"Something bothers me," Mr Lamb said.

"What?" Konstantin said over his shoulder, whilst selecting a book from the collection on a shelf.

"I don't know. It just doesn't feel right." He picked up his phone, made a call. "Meadows? I'd appreciate your help. I'm sending you a photo. I need to know everything about the person."

"Is this related to the case?" Meadows replied.

"Maybe. I'm not sure."

He received a sigh. "Okay, I'll see what I can do. Use my personal e-mail address, would you?" The Superintendent disconnected.

Mr Lamb sat on the bed, rested the laptop on his thighs, plugged the camera in, watched it sync and download the files on the memory card to the hard drive in a matter of seconds. Opened an e-mail, attached several images from different angles, typed in the address, clicked 'Send'.

It took all of five minutes to get a response.

"One Harry Piles," Mr Lamb said, reading directly from the e-mail on screen. "Relatively petty crime, from burglary upwards. Has a history of violence. Been in prison several times, once for aggravated assault. Puzzling. Not the sort of man a captain of industry would associate with."

Konstantin shrugged dismissively. He had his head in a novel. "Would you put top man on babysitting duty?"

Mr Lamb conceded that the Russian had a point. He read out some more.

"This is interesting ... Reputed to work for one Steven Oakhill."

Konstantin looked up, raised an eyebrow in a vaguely thoughtful fashion.

"Him again. If this Russia in my day, these guys be buried in snow by now."

"Or in politics," Mr Lamb said. "Or business."

Konstantin looked at Mr Lamb in surprise, said, "You make joke!"

"No, merely a factual observation. I don't think we should wait. I suggest we go in there tonight and meet Gordon Dredge. Find out what the hell is going on."

"Da," said Konstantin. "I sick of standing around. Need do something."

"We've only just got here."

"So?"

Gangster Style

Two Days Ago

After leaving Mrs Lucy's, we go to the pub. But it is dull. No life or soul in the place and oddly, neither of us feel like providing it. When we get back to the house, Lucy kisses me on the forehead and takes herself off to bed. I retrieve my laptop from the Shit Machine, then spend hours going through the files on the USB stick, convinced I must have missed something. I nod off at some point.

When I wake, the light is weakly tapping at the windows. I'm stiff from sleeping upright. It feels like going long haul to Australia in cattle class.

The laptop is on the floor, open. Must have slipped off my legs at some point. I retrieve it, prod at the keys. It's dead. I plug it into the wall, head off for a shower.

Whilst I scrub up (don't act surprised, I've appearances to keep now), I thank the do-gooders that managed to get a law passed so that we non-bill payers can still have our utilities available to waste and not compensate the hugely profitable power companies for.

I'm practically no further on than twenty four hours ago. However, it occurs to me that one action I undertook caused a disproportionate and opposite reaction – seeing Dredge.

He seems to be the constant in all of this. So I reckon it's time to go visit him again. I throw some clothes on, head downstairs.

But there is another thing. In Gowan's notes, a name kept coming up. One I'd been threatened to stay away from.

Oakhill.

A Chance Meeting

A fox paused. Sniffed the air and slunk away. The sun was beginning to climb over the horizon, the soft glow providing just enough illumination for Mr Lamb and Konstantin. They moved easily through the undergrowth, even more silent than the animal itself.

It took fifteen cautious minutes to cover the ground, checking for trips, cameras and any other counter-measures Piles may have employed.

There had been none.

Mr Lamb wasn't annoyed with the elapsed time. Better safe than sorry.

He pressed his back up against the brickwork at the rear of the house. The dark side of the moon, as far as Mr Lamb was concerned, invisible from their stakeout position. There wasn't a burglar alarm in evidence, but a silent alert routed straight into the local police station was entirely possible, so they would have to be fast.

Konstantin picked the surprisingly simple lock while Mr Lamb kept watch. Then they were inside. Mr Lamb stood still, listened. No warning signals, just the ticking of a clock and some heavy snoring.

The pair split up. Konstantin would search for any intelligence, and plant several bugs and cameras if he were able. Mr Lamb's objective was to seek Dredge. Starting downstairs.

Mr. Lamb found an expansive and largely untouched kitchen, the sink full of plates, waste bin piled up with one-person microwave meal packaging. Then a utility room, stacks of dirty clothes in the corner. Drawing room, dining room with a table that could seat twenty, and last, but not least, the study, which had the most unexpected contents.

Well, content really.

"Perhaps you would care to invite your friend to join us?" Gordon Dredge said softly. "Outside?"

Unexpected, but Mr Lamb decided to roll with the change in events.

The trio stood in a cluster, a mere two hundred yards from the house in a tiny clearing of otherwise densely packed trees. Nearby was a bench and a small, overgrown pond. Dredge, who wore pyjamas and a frayed dressing gown, threadbare slippers on his feet, seemed not to notice the cold.

"I know this place like the back of my hand," Dredge said. "Piles, on the other hand, doesn't. He'll stumble about like a heifer in a nettle patch *if* he decides to wake up. He sleeps like the dead, that man."

"Nevertheless, we should keep this brief."

"Understood. I'd obliged if you could help me."

"And what do you expect we can do for you?" Mr Lamb replied.

Dredge ran his fingers through grey, thinning hair and huffed through his nose. "I've been around unsavoury characters for enough of my life to spot a type."

Konstantin snorted. It sounded like an appreciative laugh.

"Thank you for that," Mr Lamb said.

"I didn't mean to be insulting, merely to demonstrate that we do not need to play games or circle each other. We are all wolves here."

"I not think so," Konstantin said.

"Be assured that I have destroyed as many lives as you."

"Is this pertinent?" Mr Lamb cut in before the testosterone flowed too heavily.

"Well said, sir. I assume you are aware of my identity?"

"Correct."

"But I'm in a position of weakness, for I am not in possession of your names."

"Lamb, Boryakov."

"Thank you. Now, my proposal to you." Dredge held a hand up before Konstantin could speak. "Please hear me out before we start arguing again and freeze to death out here."

Konstantin shrugged and turned away. Said over his shoulder, "I had enough. I go back to lookout point."

"Is he always like that?" Dredge asked, once the Russian had melted away into the darkness.

"Sometimes he's worse. Look, as I said, we may not have much time."

"You're right. I'm in trouble."

"Clearly. However, I do not understand why this could possibly be of interest to me. You're the sort of person I put away these days, rather than help."

Dredge laughed, low and deep. "I've been threatened so often, your words are of little consequence. The people I am stuck with aren't by any means angels either. So if it's a choice between you or them? It makes no difference, frankly."

"Again, Mr Dredge. *What do you want?*"

"To live."

"More specific, please."

Dredge sighed. "You're a precise sort of person, aren't you, Lamb?"

Mr Lamb simply returned the gaze.

"I've got myself into rather a tight corner with a Mr Oakhill. Do you know him?"

"By reputation only."

"Good. Oakhill and I go way back. Together, we've made rather a lot of money. He's funded several of my companies and received a handsome return. It was a good partnership."

"Was?"

"Yes. But it turned out my business partner was into most of the less than salubrious pastimes. Drugs, prostitution and," Dredge paused a moment, "Murder. I thought I knew Oakhill, but realised I didn't at all, until it was too late. You must think me stupid."

"Go on."

Dredge sighed, the weight of inevitability within. "Eventually, the police took an interest in him, then turned their sights on me, which was less than preferential. Reporters started sniffing around. Oakhill tried to hush them up, but one story leaked out. Investors got scared, the company hit a bad spot, and we were forced to fold. Oakhill lost a lot of money. Not that he needed it. The issue was more one of prestige. So he asset-stripped me and now I'm a virtual prisoner in my own home, with the delectable Harry Piles for a guard."

"And you want me to get you out of the hole you put yourself in?"

"Not precisely, no. That would be incredibly selfish of me." Dredge caught Mr Lamb's look. "I'm well aware that I sacrificed many people on the altar of my career and ego. But murder? I cannot condone Oakhill killing my employees just for personal gain."

"James Hollowman being one of them?"

Dredge walked over to the bench, sat down heavily, said in a barely audible voice, "Yes."

"I knew him."

"Then we have a shared objective."

"I assume these people were silenced because they saw something that they shouldn't?"

"Correct. And so have I."

"Were you aware of these occurrences?"

"Oakhill called them 'adjustments', and no, I wasn't, until the last kick of the game."

Mr Lamb watched the slumped figure. Dredge looked genuinely upset. Greedy and arrogant for sure, but not a killer.

"Okay, I will help you. But I cannot promise that you'll evade a prison sentence."

"Good enough for me."

Mr Lamb's phone vibrated.

"Harry Piles is in the grounds looking for you," he said.

"I was out for a walk."

"Will he believe you?"

"I don't care."

Mr Lamb handed over his mobile. "We'll need to talk again. Don't let Piles find it."

Dredge stood up and took the phone. He held out his hand for Mr Lamb to shake. The grip was firm. Dredge released and walked away.

For The Hell Of It

"Do you want a coffee?" Lucy shouts out of the kitchen as I head down the stairs.

"Does the Pope shit in the woods?"

Lucy's leaning against a kitchen cabinet. She blows on a cup of tea, nods towards my steaming mug.

I've never understood that. We boil water, pour it onto a bag or grains, then allow it cool it down again before swallowing it.

Why? Waste of time. Just heat it to the required temperature. Or stick to alcohol. I take a gulp of the black liquid, scald my throat.

"I'm off out," I tell Lucy through pained lips.

"Okay," she replies. Puts her tea down. "I'll come along."

I shake my head. "It'll be dangerous."

She shrugs. "Try and stop me."

I open my mouth. Close it. Pointless arguing with a woman.

She smiles, knows she's won. "Give me five minutes to get decent."

We're in the Shit Machine doing fifty. The early morning roads are free of traffic, but covered with ice. The gritters haven't been out yet. A pitch-black cloud hangs low and menacing over the horizon. It looks like snow.

I've a fag on, but the benefit of having no windows left is all the smoke is drawn away immediately. However, the denser ash blows onto my chest as I negotiate a corner.

The downside of said window-less condition? It's fucking freezing.

"Do you ever use the brake?" Lucy shouts. She's hanging on for dear life.

I shrug, grin, reply, "Told you it would be dangerous."

We grind to a halt outside Dredge's gaff. I swear to God (not really) that Lucy would be kissing the ground if it didn't mean kneeling down in the wet to do so. She leans on the car instead and beams at me wide eyed to prove, outwardly at least, that she's fine.

I start the hike to the main entrance. She can stay where she is or follow. I don't mind either way. I hammer on the door. Lucy's pops into my peripheral vision. Good girl. I have to pound away twice more before I hear shuffling movement inside.

A bleary-eyed Dredge answers. His hair is everywhere and he's in his night clothes, dressing-gown haphazard. He looks like that Cherie Blair did all those years ago, when she opened up No. 10 the morning after the biggest party of her life.

I look at my watch, tut, shake my head. "Staff got the day off?"

He tries to shut the door on me. I put out a hand, respond in kind. One shove and Dredge staggers back. He suddenly looks alert. Got a good kick up the mental arse. I waft Lucy inside as a gentleman does, then enter myself.

The hall is dim once the front door closes, but it's easy to detect that Dredge's mansion has seen better days. There's hardly a stick of furniture in it for one. Cobwebs hang down, dust covers every surface, and a pile of mail as thick as my head lurks on the floor.

"Oh dear, Gordon. Life not treating you so well?" I ask. It's hard not to smile at the arrogant bastard's apparent slide from grace.

"Fuck off," he replies. "And leave me alone, Brodie."

Two interesting items there.

First, there's no weight to his tone, no fight in the guy. Second, he knows my name.

I might learn something after all.

"With pleasure, once you tell me what I want to know." I pick up the post, thumb through with a practiced digit. "Looks like you missed a couple here, Gordon."

I pass over some red bills. He slides them into his dressing gown pocket, but doesn't appear embarrassed. His sort never do. He stares Lucy up and down, clearly unimpressed by her appearance. The natural self-confidence, born of a public-school upbringing, is beginning to reassert itself.

I continue, "I'm hoping you can help me with my article."

Dredge laughs, deep and hearty. It echoes. "Why on earth would I do that?"

"Because if you don't, I'll publish anyway."

He squints at me. Says, "What's it about?"

"You and Oakhill."

He staggers back a step or two. Like he's taken a brutal left hook. Splutters, "What … ? How did … ?"

I seem to have hit a rather raw nerve. Pure bastard luck for once.

He shouts, "Piles!"

"Medical condition troubling you, Gordon?"

He ignores me. Bellows again, "Piles! Get up, man!"

There's the sound of a thump, heavy feet hitting the floor above us. How you'd imagine a gorilla getting out of bed.

Then Harry Piles, overweight driver and general thug, waddles down the stairs in t-shirt and dirty Y-fronts.

As he descends, says through a yawn, "What do you want, you old fart?"

Dredge points. Piles follows his finger and ends up at me.

"Ready for a second beating, Harry?" I ask.

Piles grins at me. Says, "Always with the wisecracks."

I shrug. "It's an underappreciated skill, I believe."

Piles lifts his arm, a gun in hand. It's shiny and new. He looks like a shark. Says, "Not fucking joking now are you, Brodie?"

"What are you doing, Harry?" Dredge says. Looks as shocked by the turn of events as I feel.

"Okay, perhaps I've overstayed my welcome. We'll leave you alone for now, Gordon. Mr Piles, good to see you, as always."

"You're not going anywhere, mate," Piles says, grin deepening.

"I'll not have anyone killed in my house," Dredge says. "There's been enough murder." He steps between the gaping gun barrel and us. "Let them go, Harry."

"I've told you before, you can't order me around. You've no right."

Dredge drops his voice to barely a whisper, "You can't pull the trigger, Harry. Your boss would turn you into horsemeat in a heartbeat if you did."

I'm standing, open-mouthed, listening to this exchange. Harry's arm sags, the barrel sinks to target the floor.

Lucy tugs at my elbow. "Come on!" she hisses.

She's dead on.

I turn, yank open the door. The cold air punches me. A quick dash to the Shit Machine. Lucy's footfalls in the gravel just behind me. I'm pleased for once I haven't locked the car, because I'm in in moments. So is Lucy.

I turn the engine over, still praying. A pig flies overhead as the engine catches first time. I slam the car into reverse, smack down the accelerator and pelt backwards.

Brake, spin the steering wheel and crash into first gear. The car protests, but performs a ragged about-face under my coaxing hands. I glance in the rear-view mirror.

Piles barges out the front door. Takes a shooting stance, legs spread, knees bent, arms out straight. Panic and almost lose the back end in a skid, furiously spin the steering wheel in the opposite direction.

There's a *crack*! Loud even over the throaty exhaust. The wing mirror shatters. Another *crack* and I'm down the drive and out onto the main road without pausing.

I laugh, relief and adrenaline coursing through my veins. But I laugh alone.

"You ok?" I ask Lucy.

She doesn't answer.

I turn to look at her and what I see turns me to stone.

Payback

Harry Piles shoved Dredge, sent him tumbling, ignored the clap of skull on parquet. He ran outside, caught a glimpse of the car, aimed. The sight steadied. He'd been taught well. Squeezed. Went with the kick.

First bullet missed.

Piles didn't complain. Difficult to take an exact bead on the car as it slewed around on the gravel.

Took his time, focused, breathed out slowly, had a few seconds to make the shot count.

Applied a steady pressure to the trigger, was hit hard on the shoulder. The pain was as sharp as it was unexpected.

The gun went off, but fuck knows where the bullet ended up. Struck again, shoulder stung as if nibbled by a wasp. Piles span, faster than a big man should.

Dredge, blood coursing from a cut on his forehead, walking cane raised over his shoulder to assault a third time. As he swung the stick down, Harry put out a hand. Stopped it mid-trajectory. Snapped it in two, the sound dry and rotten.

Harry smiled, punched Dredge. The old man went down heavily again. Turned back to target Brodie's car, but those precious few moments were wasted, never to be reclaimed. He was out of sight.

"Fuck!" Harry bellowed.

He kicked the prone Dredge in the ribs. Lifted his foot a second time, thought better of it. He couldn't waste more time. Harry stormed back into the house. Ignored the sound of Dredge vomiting.

Needed to make a call. The boss was going to be furious.

Mr Lamb lowered the binoculars, couldn't believe his eyes. He recognised the man Piles had been shooting at and decided that Brodie had risen to the top of the list of people to speak to.

Then his phone rang.

A Vague Recollection

I drive even more erratically than usual. My heart is in my mouth, breathing sharp and shallow. It feels like there's a shortage of oxygen despite the wind that's blasting through the absent windows.

I keep glancing over at Lucy, eyes more on her than the road. She lolls with the car's motion. I've no idea if she's unconscious or dead. I'm desperate to check, but at the same time afraid of what I may find.

First, though, it's essential to put enough distance between us and Harry Piles. He could be somewhere out here now, cruising around in the Bentley, gun handy.

Bullet between the eyes.

So I need to find somewhere secluded, pull up. It's a fine balance between personal safety and survival of a friend. I catch myself. Almost fly off the bend.

Friend? Did I *really* mean that? I haven't had a proper one of those in a while. Haven't wanted one either. Too dangerous.

I spot somewhere. A secluded lay-by. Behind a line of trees. Not brilliant, as they're largely bereft of leaves, but better than nothing. At least the branches should blur anyone's view as they drive past at speed.

Primarily, though, I can't put it off any longer. The Shit Machine skids a little as I brake too hard. A police car flashes by, blues and twos going ten to the dozen. I duck, but they're too interested in getting to where they're going.

I lean over to check Lucy. No seat belt as an encumbrance, as I didn't clunk-click whilst Harry Piles was raining bullets down on us.

Press my finger on her neck. Pulse. There's a pulse. I can feel the vein throbbing. It's strong, regular, repetitive.

Thank fuck.

I feel around her body to see if I can detect any blood. None. Then I notice a cleave along the side of her head. It looks like the bullet brushed past, skimming the skull. She'd been bare millimetres from expiration.

One thing's for sure, she'll have a banging headache when she wakes.

She groans.

"Lucy?"

Her head comes up, attempts to focus on me. Her neck isn't quite strong enough to take the weight. Looks as though she's drunk. Or just been shot.

"Did you try and cop a quick feel, you dirty bastard?" she asks.

I hold my hands up in surrender.

I'm at my house. Lucy in the Shit Machine, engine wheezing. I sprint in and up the stairs. Toss her clothes in her bag, add a few of my own on top. Get the critical things like the laptop, cash and the coffee pot.

I'm back out again inside sixty seconds, leaving the door yawning open behind me. It's only a building, bad memories within. My only regret is having to leave my chair behind. Maybe I'll be able to reclaim it when all this is over.

The wheels don't squeal as I pull away, no tread left, but the Shit Machine shifts it.

I head for a B&B I know. I stayed there with the missus when we were looking for the holiday home. It's small, discrete, tucked out the way. I'm on nodding terms with the owners which helps as well.

Five minutes of furious driving gets me there. Two more minutes and we're in the room. It's pretty basic – bed, chair, wardrobe, kettle, television. Glad I brought the coffee pot.

A quick trip to the local superstore, head down and walking in the shadows, get some supplies and I'm back in a flash.

"Take these." I hand Lucy a couple of serious painkillers, the strongest I could buy without going illegal. Not that I wouldn't. It's pure expediency that's sent me on the straight and narrow drugs route. She swallows some ice cold water to hasten the tablet's descent. Coughs.

"Ah, fuck that hurts," she complains. I can't blame her really. I guess bullets tend to sting.

She's sitting up on the bed, rests her head back against the pile of pillows.

"I'll try not to make it any worse, okay?"

She nods, pain cutting across her brow again as she does so. I lift back her hair to look closer at the wound.

The bullet has scored a stripe across the right side of her skull, taking away a line of hair and the tip of her ear. It doesn't look bad, just angry. Bit like me. The searing heat of the bullet appears to have cauterised the wound.

"We can't go to the hospital," I tell her. "You'd get reported and the cops would be all over us in moments, asking all sorts of questions."

"Okay," Lucy says.

"I need to put some of this on." I show her the pack of ointment. She struggles to focus on it. I hope it's just from pain and not concussion.

"Okay," she whispers.

I apply the cream, as carefully as I can with my lack of male tenderness and minimal digit dexterity. She winces periodically. I think I'll have to go out again and get some gauze for her ear, but I'm no doctor.

"Bed for you, young lady," I say, once my ministrations are concluded.

"Are you trying it on again?"

"Scouts honour," I say, two fingers tapping my forehead in mock salute despite having not been the former and possessing none of the latter.

"Can you come with me, please? I don't want to be left on my own."

I want to say no, but I can see the need in her eyes. She's already been hurt once today. I can't do it again to her.

So, against better judgement, I clamber in beside to her. Fewer clothes than last time, but still enough to cover the erogenous zones and hide involuntary dribbles. Lucy lies on her back for a moment, then rolls onto her side, shuffles her body back into mine. I curl an arm over, all protective like, but it feels wrong ...

Troon

Mr Lamb looked at his phone. It was ringing. Not unusual, you might think. However, only Konstantin had the number, and he was lying on the bed, snoring.

He answered. Puzzlement was quickly dispelled and he agreed to meet DCI Troon.

A Lucky Escape

After an hour, Lucy's sufficiently away to her bed, sleeping as soundly as you can having had a near-death experience, so I can safely rise without waking her. She's tough, but as she's the product of Mrs Lucy, I can't say I'm surprised.

As a result, I'm sitting in the one chair this room possesses. It's not comfortable, the pattern's horrible. I feel a pang of mournful loss for my own. The room is dark. I have curtains. It's been a while.

I take a hit of vodka. Another essential supply picked up during the recent trolley dash. It's a bit warm for my liking, but it'll have to do. I'm thinking, but I can't say I like my thoughts. About the girl in bed.

It's not good getting close to people. Take it as advice from a fully paid up and totally pissed off member of the been there, seen it, loathed it brigade.

Women. Relationships. Responsibility.

All three are beautiful, brutal things, able to kill you, yet keep you alive and in suffering.

Sometimes I wonder if the female of the species are the work of the Devil, Hell on earth itself. Or God (a.k.a. He Who Doesn't Really Exist) has a particularly twisted sense of humour. Or they're in cahoots.

Some fifty proof spirit clears out the bullshit thoughts of the present, but the past wells up instead …

I met the missus (let's keep names out of it, we live in a litigious society after all) in the strangest of fashions.

I'm in my flat, minding my own business, when there's a knock at the door. Which is odd, because I live on the top floor, four more residences beneath me.

So there's a pounding. I'm frowning because I don't understand the sound, well not in the context at least.

It comes again, so I get up, open the door a crack. There's a woman standing there, a bit demure, not exactly brimming with confidence. Not stunning, not ugly, but nevertheless the owner of squidgy bits.

Then I do it. I utter the stupidest four words ever. If I could go back in time, I'd throw my body out of the window there and then.

"Can I help you?"

To cut a long story short, she stays at my place because she has nowhere else to go. Back then I was too soft and naive. I don't ask why she was out on the street. I still don't know the reason to this day.

We meet, marry, separate. An identical situation to 50% of the population.

Unfortunately, several little offspring complicate matters so the courts get involved. Access rights denied, but I'm allowed to pay my money to them, so that's something at least.

Was it deliberate? Maybe.

Therefore I cannot get close to anyone again, particularly a member of the opposite sex. It didn't end well last time, it won't this time.

Lucy seems like a decent girl, but again I discover someone appearing in my life in the strangest of circumstances, who wants to be close in the merest of moments.

And already I've managed to get her hurt.

The bedside lamp clicks on. I blink in the sudden, relative brightness. Lucy's sitting up, squinting at me.

We'd undressed in the dark. I try not to notice her underwear. Skimpy, lacy, black. She has well-defined lines, obviously worked out a lot.

The weald along her skull is a livid red and a little lost in the midst of her ginger hair.

"You okay?" she says.

"It's me should be asking you that," I say, feel guilty.

She shrugs, twitches an eyebrow to state, *You haven't answered my question.*

I say, "Just thinking."

"I can see." Lucy points to the vodka bottle resting in my lap. "Is it worth it?"

"What?" I frown, puzzled.

"Thinking."

"Actually, most of the time, no."

"Pass me the bottle then," she says. "Let's not think together."

Dredge Regrets

Gordon Dredge felt his leg vibrate. It was the phone the man called Lamb had given him. It hadn't left his possession since the fated meeting in the woods.

Dredge knew it was a potential lifeline if it remained undiscovered, but a noose if it was.

He bolted out of his chair, trotted across the study, pushed the door closed (although he couldn't lock it as all the keys had been themselves sealed in a safe).

Dredge pulled the mobile out of his pocket. The connection dropped.

"Balls!" he grated under his breath.

Almost immediately, the phone jangled in his hand again. Dredge immediately pressed the green key in case it rang off a second time.

He placed the receiver against his ear, moved across to some French windows that looked out over his land. They also happened to be the point in the room furthest from the door.

"Lamb?" he said, keeping his voice as low as possible.

"Yes. I assume you can speak?"

"Briefly."

"I'll keep it short, then. Do you know what Oakhill wants with you?"

"He's going to turn me out on the street sometime soon."

"Are you ever left alone?"

"Rarely, although Piles has to sleep periodically. I'm essentially kept in almost total isolation."

There was a moment's silence on the other end of the line. Dredge looked over his shoulder.

The study door remained closed. He was just being paranoid. Elephants were lighter on their feet than Dirty Harry.

He heard a whisper in his ear. "What was all the commotion about earlier today?"

Dredge almost laughed. *Commotion*. Such an innocuous word for almost extreme violence.

"A reporter came calling."

"Brodie."

"Yes."

"What was he interested in?"

"Me. And Oakhill. I've had trouble with him in the past. But Harry took umbrage to his presence and concluded matters in a rather robust and abrupt fashion."

"Do you know someone by the name of Meadows?"

Dredge stopped breathing.

Gordon raised a glass to Harry Piles when he entered the study five minutes later.

A frown creased the big man's brow. He said, "I've told you before, old man. Leave this open."

"Of course, Harry." Dredge smiled. "Whatever you say."

Piles' frown deepened, but he buggered off once he was satisfied Dredge wasn't up to anything. The false smile fell off Dredge's face. He thought back to the shooting, felt like he'd righted a wrong.

Despite the impression he'd given Brodie yesterday, he remembered him very well. The man was seared into his memory. How could he not be? Damn near ruined him. The reporter had got very, very close to the truth and Dredge, in a fit of desperation, had had to bring Oakhill in.

But with terrible consequences. It'd all been a disaster. The reporter's subsequent fall from grace was the least of events. People had died. Good people.

Hollowman he'd only recently known, but the others – they had long been colleagues. They'd worked together, broken bread together. More importantly, made money together. That was something you never forget.

A year ago, he'd blamed Brodie. Decided the fallout was entirely on his shoulders. Whatever the washed up reporter got, he deserved.

But recently, since he'd gone into an enforced retirement, Gordon had had plenty of time to think. His conscience (remarkably he had one) told him Brodie had done nothing but sniff out the dirty truth.

"Christ, what a mess," Dredge said out loud.

He hoped he'd told the man Lamb enough. Because in his heart, he knew the end was near.

Wondered if he could justify his actions when the reckoning came.

Lamb Chops

I awake a little later. It doesn't feel like either of us has moved since we first made contact with the mattress.

Lucy remains in a foetal position and pulled into me. Although I'm in t-shirt and boxers, there's far too much skin contact for comfort. I extract myself slowly in what's becoming a habitual process.

It's when the kettle boils that I realise I didn't bring any coffee with me, so I throw some clothes on and make a repeat trip to the local store to amend the monumental oversight.

I'm on the way back when my phone rings. I don't recognise the number. I'm getting pretty fed up with people trying to communicate with me. I think I preferred it when no-one liked me.

"David Brodie?" the voice drifts over the line. Accentless, unremarkable, but shit-arse scary for a reason I can't define.

"How did you get this number? Only about five people have it."

"I've contacts, David. Wholly unsavoury ones, but incredibly resourceful. A mere telephone number? Child's play, I assure you."

"Who is this?"

"I'm known as Mr Lamb to some."

"Sounds inappropriate," I say, thinking it's a good way to break the ice. The guy's giving me the utter creeps. Shits and giggles usually work on the scary ones. They don't.

"And you would be totally correct," Lamb says, cold water dousing my misplaced humour. "I understand you are aware of Gordon Dredge."

"Another inappropriate statement," I say. Steel in my tone.

"Quite. I've just been reading the back story. It's rather something."

"Look, what do you want?"

"I've been speaking to Dredge. He's been very … revealing. I believe I can help you fill in some of the blanks."

"Well that would be a first."

"Possibly. Where could we meet?"

Orders Are Orders

More than anything, Lucy wanted sleep, to settle into total unconsciousness. To awake only once everything was over. But it wasn't to be. Her head hurt. The crease along her skull felt like it was on fire. Worse still, her heart ached.

She opened her eyes as soon as David left the room, scrabbled for the phone, dialled, spoke.

Was asked a question she didn't want to answer.

But did so.

Hated herself for it.

Orders were orders after all.

Snatch

My jaw is halfway to forming a reply when a white van draws up. The rear doors burst open before it's entirely stopped. Two men jump out. I still have the phone to my ear, but I can't hear Lamb anymore.

In the merest of moments, I'm bundled inside and the vehicle is rolling. The interior is plain, featureless and smells of cake.

I'm on my knees, swaying with the motion of the vehicle. One of the bastards nicks my mobile, listens, grunts, disconnects. Three men face me, seated on benches screwed into the wall. Two familiar, one not at all.

"Who's been fucking stupid then?" says Skinhead from the pub a couple of nights ago. The pair of black eyes and tape across the bridge of his nose alters his appearance from the last time we met.

"Looks nasty," I say.

As Skinhead scrunches a fist and I clench my buttocks, the man I've never met before speaks. "Hold it."

He's big, powerful, used to being in control and liking it. Shaved head, leather jacket, sovereigns on most of his fingers.

"For fuck's sake, boss. Just one little tap. Please?" Skinhead pleads in a whiny voice.

"Touch him and you'll answer to Stevie."

I assume he means Oakhill, the guy I was warned off. Decide I may learn something, provided I don't end up a vegetable in the next few minutes.

Skinhead's paw drops. The big man bangs on the wall, right behind the driver's head. We immediately slow, stop.

"Get out, both of you," the big guy orders.

"What?" Skinhead replies.

"I hate repeating myself. People get hurt when I repeat myself."

I decide it's wisest not to point out he's just made a contradictory statement.

Skinhead slithers out, closely followed by his mate. Doors close softly behind them. The van rocks as they get into the cab. Big guy bangs on the wall. We're off again.

"Just you and me now, Brodie."

I say, "My luck has always been shit."

He doesn't laugh.

Fat Chance

Mr Lamb pressed mute, listened to the commotion over the speaker. Recognised the sounds of a snatch squad. There was the sound of some heavy breathing, like the person had a nasal problem, then a grunt and the line was cut off.

Someone had Brodie.

Lucy lay back, thinking. Her head was pounding. Her phone rang again. She grabbed it, said, "David?"

"No, unfortunately not. My name is Mr Lamb."

"Christ, I've heard of you."

"I'm sorry, but time is wasting. I believe your Mr Brodie has been snatched."

Lucy's head span. So much had happened in the last twenty four hours. Said, "By who?"

"I suspect a Mr Oakhill will be behind it all."

"Shit!"

"Where are you? I'll come and pick you up."

Lucy tossed her bag in the boot, sat in the front next to Lamb.

"Any idea where they'll be holding him?" Lucy asked.

Mr Lamb shook his head. "Impossible to know. I don't have the intel on their set-up. You?"

She shook her head, tried to call David again. No answer. Lucy gnawed on the tip of her thumb, stared out the window.

Mr Lamb began cruising the streets in a grid pattern, up and across. There were hundreds, probably thousands in the surrounding area. He knew the chances of finding David were tiny, but they had to try.

He was probably in deep shit.

A Word Of Advice

I pretty certain I'm in deep shit. The big guy just glares at me until a little smirk creeps over his lips.

"Do you know who I am?" he says.

"Clueless."

Smirk turns into a grin, like he knows that already. Says, "Park your arse."

I do as he tells me. Clamber up off my knees, stagger a bit as we go round a corner, land heavily on the bench.

We rock around for a minute, on our opposite sides, staring each other out. Part of me yells, "*Danger!*", but it's like facing down a wild animal – displaying fear is more hazardous to health than feigning strength.

"I'd heard you're a clever bastard, or used to be at any rate. Until your … little sexual problem."

That again.

"Look, is there some specific aim to this? Because I can get criticised in any one of a hundred places."

"I'm sure." He stuffs out a shovel-sized hand, takes me by surprise. "Frank McGavin." We shake, because no man can resist doing so. I hear my knuckles crack. Try not to whimper.

"I'm still pissed about you guys doing over my car."

Frank shrugs, like it's a minor misdemeanour. Which it probably is.

He says, "No idea what you're talking about."

"Right." I don't believe him.

"We're on our way to see Stevie."

"The great man. Am I supposed to be impressed?"

"I'd suggest worried instead. Or shitting yourself. Either one is better than being a smart arse. Good to see you're being true to form."

"You know nothing about me."

"Wrong. I know *everything* about you."

We eyeball each other again. Frank hangs on to the bench as we swerve, pick up speed.

"You haven't figured it out yet, have you?" he says.

I'm lost, just shrug like it's an irrelevance.

"The stuff from Gowan. I gave it to you."

"There was nothing I didn't already know."

"For fuck's sake, Brodie. There was a whole seam of shit to mine in there, and you missed it." He shakes his head.

"If you say so."

"Did you look on the stick?"

"What stick?"

Frank sighed. "I'm trying to do you a favour here, Brodie. Do you want the story? Get yourself back in the news?"

Of course I want the story. More than that, it's essential I have it. Or I stay a nothing forever.

"Maybe."

"Then wise the fuck up."

"Okay, if you say so. Is that it? Can I go now?"

Frank laughs, a short bark.

"Not a chance. I wasn't lying when I said I'm taking you to see my boss." He sighs. Frustration evident. "Look, Stevie is going to push you hard. Keep it shut. Don't wind him up. He's on a knife edge at the best of times and you've got a smart mouth on you."

"And you'll tell me what the hell is going on here?"

"Sure. Just not a word to anyone, your bird included."

"She's not my bird."

"Whatever. There's something else we've got to do."

"What?"

"This …" and Frank punches me.

Lights out.

My jaw hurts. So does my head, because someone is lifting it by my hair and slapping me none to gently in the face.

"Fucking wake up." A voice that's forty fags and a bottle of gin a day.

"Do I have to?"

"Pop your peepers."

"Eh?"

Peepers popped, I see there's an ugly, pimply-faced bastard holding my hair. Big teeth and a scowl.

There's Frank, with all his bulk, and standing a few feet away from him is a man molehill. Short, powerful, well dressed. And glaring at me with a radioactive intensity.

I've two choices. Fight. Or flight. Fuck it, go on the offensive.

"Who are you?" I ask.

Frank narrows his eyes. I'm already ignoring his advice.

But my comment merely generates laughter in the room. Apparently, I should know who I'm dealing with.

"He's asking who you are, boss," says the guy with the teeth.

"Yeah, Squirrel, I heard." The guy shakes his head, like Squirrel is an idiot.

"The man is Stevie The Steroid Oakhill," Squirrel says.

"Fuck," I reply.

"Yeah," he replies, all Northern bastard-like. "Fuck is right, old son."

He takes a chair, a wooden one like my grandma used to have in her kitchen, holds it horizontal in both hands. For a moment I think he's going to hit me with it. Or split it in two.

But he does neither.

After a heartbeat, Stevie plants it down opposite me and sits, leans back, massive arms folded. He doesn't request permission, just does it. I suspect it's been a long time since he's checked with anyone first before making a decision.

Steroid hasn't blinked once. He's very still, very intense. Like he might go postal any moment. Keeps his grey eyes fixed on me.

Eventually, he says, "Why did you go and see Dredge?"

I shrug. "For a laugh. See what he'd do."

He grins at me. "Clever fucker, aren't you?"

I respond in kind. Couldn't care less what he thinks. What you don't have can't be taken away from you. All that stuff about having to stay alive just long enough to get revenge?

Bullshit.

Once you've stopped breathing and your heart's still, there's nothing as far as I'm concerned. So you're not going to know any better. Dead is fucking dead.

"If you want to do it, Stevie, just go ahead. I'm not exactly enamoured with my shitty life."

He peers at me, clearly deciding whether it's front or not. I stare back.

"Okay, you're obviously a thick bastard. Normally by now, people I sit down with are falling over themselves to tell me how they can help me. In fact, before I've even laid me hand on a chair, they cock-a-doodle-doo."

I shrug. "Why would I want to help you?"

He laughs. Short, guttural, very fucking unpleasant.

"One more chance. Why did you go and see Dredge?" he asks.

I don't reply.

Stevie sighs, nods to one of his men, the black eyed skinhead. He walks over to me.

I don't bother trying to evade him. I can't, what with being bound tightly to a chair. He smoothes a lock of my hair behind my right ear. I try to bite him but miss and get backhanded.

The room spins for a few moments. When my vision clears, I can see a few drops of blood on my lap. The room is quiet except for the faint sound of water dripping. We're probably miles away from anyone and anywhere.

"Last chance," Stevie whispers into the silence.

I can barely hear him. Say, "So the other last chance was in fact the penultimate one."

Stevie nods to Skinhead, takes my hand, snaps my little finger.

At first, nothing.

Then the worst pain I've ever experienced floods up my arm. I scream, can't help myself. It fucking hurts. I breathe deeply, head down, fight the waves of pain that break over me. Eventually, it recedes enough for me to look up and into Stevie's eyes.

He laughs lightly, leans in and pats me on the cheek all friendly. Like we're old comrades. The guy's nuts. Says, "Look, if you're no threat to me, I'll let you go. You have my word on that. We're just here for a bit of a chat is all."

Yeah, right. I'm tied up. No-one knows where I am. None of his men are going to talk if I end up dead. He sees the look of doubt splash across my face.

"You can trust me," Stevie says.

The skinhead sniggers, Steroid twists his head, glares at him. The smirk drops off his face quicker than a whore's drawers.

I give in. "Okay, but I don't have much to say."

"Sensible."

"I guess you know all about my past history with our mutual friend?"

Stevie nods, looking more intense if at all possible. "Yeah, yeah. Not interested in the deceased past."

Sigh, drop my head again. Stare at the blood still dripping from my nose, decide I don't have a lot of choice. Carry on talking, "It's not what you think. I've had no luck with stories recently. With life, really. Since Dredge. I'd been trying to get on with it. But then some guy I'd never heard of rang the mobile the other day, said he had something for me. He just mentioned Dredge. And that was enough. He had me hooked. I had nothing to lose, so I met him. He told me some unlikely tale about Dredge and gave me a file. But apparently he's dead and the file's gone. So I've nothing material. I thought I'd just scare the old bastard, see if something came out."

Stevie stares at me through slits. "Where's the file? You lost it or something?"

"No. Someone turned my house over. It was there before, gone after."

"Did you read it?"

"No. It was stolen before I had chance." Which strictly isn't a lie.

"Sounds and smells like bullshit."

"It wasn't you that broke in?"

Oakhill laughs his laugh again. "If it were me, I'd know everything I needed to and you wouldn't be strapped to a chair shitting in your pants."

He has a point.

"Okay, boys, how do you suggest we put this one out of his misery? Fast or slow?" Oakhill says.

Just then a mobile rings. As is the way, everyone looks at everyone else, assuming it's not theirs but patting pockets anyway.

"It's you," I say.

Frank grunts, answers the call. "Yeah, what?" He listens briefly, ends the call without saying another word. Lights a fag and pulls on it like his life depends on the nicotine.

He snorts out a cloud of grey smoke, looks fit to burst with barely contained rage. His face is red. It's come out of nowhere. Says, "Have you got a moment, boss?"

Bacterial Warfare

"Let him go? For fuck's sake, what are you on about?" Oakhill raged.

Frank wondered if the shouting could be heard through the walls. They were standing in a small office, just up the corridor from where the reporter was tied up and bleeding. He knew the smart move would be to stroke Stevie's incredibly large ego, make him feel like a king, but he couldn't help himself. Frank was sick of bending to a man who was lesser than he and had been for years.

However, Stevie looked fit to blow a gasket, and Frank wondered whether he'd miscalculated by pulling him out in front of everyone. He'd have to tread very, very carefully.

"Boss, he's a reporter. They're like germs. They breed, there's millions of the bastards."

"Then who gives a shit about one less?"

"Think of it another way. One disappears, three more appear, sniffing out the story. Then eight, then you've got ... anyway, loads of 'em. More than we want hanging around here, desperate to earn some money by digging up a story. We ain't the IRA. We can't just keep knocking names off every five minutes and expect no-one will ever wise up to it. We've done enough of that already."

Frank could see Stevie was thinking. He shut up for a minute. Always best to let him believe every idea was his.

"Okay, keep convincing me." Stevie leant against a wall. It sagged slightly. No wonder the place was condemned.

Frank had hoped he'd already said enough. Clearly not.

Stevie was making him sweat because of the outburst.

He swallowed. Said, "Well, erm we might find out a bit more by following them. You know, learn what he's up to, like."

"And?"

"Well, that's it, really."

Stevie rubbed chin, stubble rasped, stared at Frank without blinking. The moments stretched. So did Frank's sphincter.

"Okay, I like it. Decent thinking, Frank."

"Thanks, boss." Frank sighed inwardly with relief.

"But, publicly embarrass me like that again and I'll cut your fucking balls off and shove 'em down your throat. Got me?"

Frank nodded.

"Good. Go tell him it's his lucky day."

"Thick bastard," Frank heard Stevie mumble as the office door was closing.

Trash Or Treasure

With the top echelon gone, no-one quite knows what to do with themselves, lost without instructions and clearly no precedence on which to make decisions. They stand around. Squirrel farts. Skinhead glares at him.

I can hear shouting, but no distinct words. The boys stare at each other, shrug. Skinhead lights up, looks bored. The door opens, Frank re-enters. Alone.

He says to me, "You know what? It's your lucky day, kid. I'm going to let you run a little longer. But be careful. I've got you on a very short leash." Frank turns to Squirrel. "Get him out of here."

"You sure?" Squirrel asks.

Frank slowly brings his vision onto the offending character. "It's a fucking good job for you, son, that I'm in a good mood."

Squirrel swallows. I can hear the gulp from where I'm sitting.

"Next time you ask me a question, you're dead. Understand?"

Squirrel nods vigorously.

"So why aren't you fucking moving, then?"

He fucking moves.

Squirrel and Skinhead load me into the back of a white van, still tied to the chair. Literally. Like I'm a piece of junk.

The doors slam and I'm alone. The interior of this one stinks of rotted fish. I want to gag.

Nothing happens for half a minute, then the vehicle rocks as someone clambers into the cab. Doors slam. Engine turns over, catches and purrs. Without warning, we set off. I slide along the floor, heading towards the rear.

We go around a corner and I tip over, landing heavily on my shoulder. I bump around like a sack of crap for far too long. I'm bruised to buggery all over. My finger stings.

Before long, we slide to a stop – in other words, my head concludes my slither when the van halts. The top of my skull cracks into the door. There's a peal of car horns. Someone's not happy.

The pressure on my cranium is relieved a moment later, when the doors open. Strong, cold, wonderful air and weak sunlight flood in.

Maybe my last? Maybe not.

The pair unceremoniously drag my carcass outside, fly-tip me. Skinhead slaps me on the cheek, grins at me.

"See you later, fuckhead," he says.

They get back into the van. Gears crash and I'm left behind in a puff of smoke.

Okay, I'm free and I'm still breathing but, the problem? Besides still being bound to the chair, I'm marooned in the middle of a dual carriageway.

Some guy walks past with a yappy dog.

"You all right over there?" he shouts. I can barely understand him. Broad Scottish accent (think Trainspotting, subtitles not included). A car buzzes between us, not helping matters.

"Yeah, fine thanks!"

The guy waves at me, says, "Aye, right you are then." And buggers off with the mutt at his feet.

"Oh, for fuck's sake."

The road isn't busy at this precise moment, but I know that won't last.

I can't wait for a Good Samaritan to stop and help me, I'll have to take things into my own hands. I rock the chair from side to side. It's not too difficult, it's precarious already.

A couple of heavy lunges and I'm over. I land on my arm. Broken finger explodes in pain, head sings for a few moments.

I'd been expecting to hear the crack of wood, i.e. the chair shattering under gravity, as happens in the movies. But I'm mortally disappointed. It's still in one piece although, the way things are looking, I may not be. This is because I'm half on, half off the road. There's one positive aspect – my arse is on double yellow lines, so at least no-one will park on me.

The bigger concern is the car that's just dropped off the roundabout and is gathering pace now it's on the straight and narrow.

I shut my eyes, wonder who I'll see on the other side once I'm dead. Then remember I don't believe in all that stuff. Try and switch off from imminent expiration, but my ears are still open. I can hear the car getting closer, the sound of rubber on tarmac. There's a knocking from the exhaust and then a screech as the brakes are applied, hard.

The idling of an engine, the repetitive tick of hazard lights, the smell of exhaust fumes. Perhaps I've shit myself, I'm not sure.

I pop an eyelid. It's dark, but that's because the bumper is above my head. Someone grabs the chair and hauls me out, pulls me upright. A middle-aged guy.

"Would you like some help?" he says.

This time I avoid sarcasm, simply say, "Yes. Please."

Coppers Stick Together

Lucy's phone rang. Mr Lamb watched out the corner of his eye as she stabbed at the green key to answer it. Saw relief flood across her face. It was puzzling, seemed extreme. But then human emotion was an anathema to him.

"David? Oh, thank God! Where are you?" Lucy listened briefly. "Okay, we'll be there in a few minutes."

Lucy told him where to go. As Mr Lamb executed a three point turn, his own phone rang.

"Yes?" he said.

"Ah, Lamb, Governor Field here. Ian Culpepper has made a request to see you."

"Tell him I'll be there in an hour."

"You owe me a favour, though."

"Why's that?"

"Prisoners are only allowed one visitor a day and I've given you priority."

"Over who?"

"Can't say I'm afraid, but it's one on the side of the angels. They're in law enforcement, like you."

Meet Mr Lamb

Five minutes later and a car pulls up. Driven by some bloke I half recognise, but don't get much chance to see, as Lucy is out of her seat in a flash, giving me a huge hug, planting kisses all over my face. It's a bit embarrassing.

The driver blows his horn, taps his watch.

Lucy gets into the back, providing me with the passenger seat. Barely have I got my belt on, and we're pulling away. My rescuer stares straight ahead, concentrating on the road as he maintains a measured pace, just below the speed limit. He's wearing driving gloves for fuck's sake. And, I swear, he never blinks.

"I'm Mr Lamb," he says.

A memory stirs. From yesterday, a couple of days ago. It feels like longer. "We've met before," I say.

"Yes. The funeral."

"What an amazing coincidence." I don't even try to keep the sarcasm out of my voice.

"You're not the only person interested in Gordon Dredge."

"What's your involvement?"

"We've plenty of time to discuss that on the road."

"Where to?"

"Prison. And then you'll be staying with me, at a friend's house."

"I don't think so," I say. Look out the windscreen. Barely see the houses flipping by. We pull onto a main road, heading out of town.

He turns his lamp-like eyes on me. "I insist. It's the safest place for you."

"I've no idea who you are, who you're working with. Why would I trust you?"

"And what other alternative do you have?" he says quietly.

Lucy lays a hand on my shoulder as severe irritation is about to kick in. She says, "Just let Mr Lamb take us there, David. I trust him."

"Well, I don't."

"Please, for me."

I sigh. "Okay, if you say so. But our stuff's at the hotel."

Those unblinking orbs turn on me again. "Lucy brought everything with her. She's a resourceful woman."

We stop briefly at a chemist. I sit in the back seat now. Lucy binds my damaged finger whilst we drive and I talk about my day. Then Mr Lamb gives me the details of his investigation to date. Very interesting, but it gets me no nearer the truth. I suspect he's not telling me everything.

Then I wonder, who awaits us in prison?

One Banker's Redemption

Mr Lamb sat in the same room, not for the first time awaiting Ian Culpepper's arrival. Finally, he shuffled inside, laptop and folder clasped to his chest, sheepish apology stitched onto his face. The guard closed the door, rattled keys in the lock.

"Good of you to see me," Culpepper said. "I think I have something."

"Quick work," Mr Lamb observed.

"Once you know what you're looking for, it's pretty straightforward really."

Mr Lamb blinked. Culpepper and modesty weren't usually present in the same room together.

The ex-banker pulled out a chair, perched on its lip at the simple table. He lifted the laptop lid, flipped open the folder. The latter contained the financial documents Mr Lamb had left behind so recently. There were markings in biro all over it. Circles, stars, arrows joining one transaction to another.

Looked complex, but was probably simple.

"What have you found?" Mr Lamb asked.

"Your initial assumption, that there was a money laundering transaction underway, was correct. See here, here and here." Culpepper pointed at the paperwork. "Large deposits which are then transferred out, followed by similar, but crucially smaller, quantities, shifted back from a different organisation. Bad money being moved through legitimate businesses, the dubious background being squeezed out like juice from a lemon."

"So, if I understand correctly, you can trace the source of all of these transactions?"

"Mostly. It's incredibly difficult, but the breadcrumbs are there if you know how to look. There are probably a handful of people in the world that would be able to decipher this. Frankly, you're lucky to have access to me. But to answer your question, all the transactions have gone through shell companies which themselves are owned by a variety of other companies, meaning the true shareholders are entirely hidden."

"There's no way of precisely knowing who owns what?"

"Permit me to explain how it works. Money laundering typically operates in three stages." Culpepper raised his fist and counted them off. "One, cash is introduced into the financial system in some way. This is called placement or immersion. Two, complex financial transactions are undertaken to camouflage the illegal source of the cash. This is called layering or heavy soaping. Three, acquire wealth from the transactions of the illicit funds, called integration. Are you following me?"

"Go on," nodded Mr Lamb.

"Good. Well, there are placement methods." Culpepper stood up and began to pace as he spoke. "But the major ones include structuring, also called smurfing." He smiled. "There's a legal requirement to report cash movements over a certain level, so the money is divided up into smaller amounts to avoid suspicion. The launderer could also purchase bearer instruments, such as money orders, and deposit these, again avoiding the reporting regulations."

"Okay," said Mr Lamb.

Culpepper continued, apparently not hearing the interruption, he was so focused on his lecture.

"Then there's smuggling. I'm sure you know what that is."

"Of course."

Culpepper displayed a thin smile. "Then you'll be aware it's the physical movement of cash from one country to another, where there's greater secrecy, such as Switzerland, or fewer rules, say, The Caymans. Just like in the films, it's usually a man with a suitcase doing the deed.

"In a similar vein, there's round-tripping. The money is deposited in an offshore tax haven, again where record-keeping is poor, and then the cash is returned as a foreign direct investment which doesn't accrue any tax. All quite neat. Tax havens are a massive problem for governments. A couple of years ago, it was estimated the US was losing $100 billion dollars a year."

$100 billion. Mr Lamb could hardly believe his ears. But Culpepper had already moved on.

"You could also utilise a business to receive the money and then deposit both legitimate and illegal funds into its accounts, claiming all of it as genuine earnings. These are typically companies which provide a cash driven service, but have no variable costs making discrepancies hard to detect. The problem is, they're at the seedy end of the market – strip clubs, casinos, or those beauty salons, so they tend to be rather obvious targets for law enforcement agencies.

"Finally, because disclosure isn't mandatory, the true owner of the money can be disguised via trusts or shell companies."

"In other words, the criminals have lots of options open to them."

"Oh, there are more still!"

Mr Lamb held his hand up. "No, really, I've heard plenty." Culpepper looked a little crestfallen at this. "So, how do we get to the end of the piece of string?"

"We follow the money trail. Ask the question, who will profit as a result of the activity? It can be dangerous, though. These days, there are whole government organisations tracking the financial footprints of terrorists. Investigating mere corrupt politicians or criminals is very much secondary these days."

"The funds in KO Ventures amounts to what? A couple of million?"

Culpepper smiled. "£135 million actually." He spoke as if it were an everyday quantity. "Mere pocket change for a Russian oligarch. Or an investment bank." Culpepper let the revelation sink in, then said, "But there's one problem. Some data is missing."

"What do you mean?"

"I mean the file is incomplete. It's difficult to spot, only an expert would be able to pick up on it. Some of the information has been culled. The maths doesn't quite add up. Someone appears to have made an attempt to cover up a number of transactions. They've done a very good job of it."

"Do you know who?"

Culpepper shook his head. "Unfortunately, no. There are some details, but not enough." He pointed at a curtailed string of numbers, circled in red several times. "Find who owns that account, you've more than likely got your man."

Mr Lamb looked up at Culpepper, saw him grinning like an idiot.

Stevie disconnected the call. He was in shorts and a vest, had a towel round his thick neck. He'd been pumping iron. With most people, this burned energy off. Not Stevie. The activity generated extra. He was his own little dynamo.

Sweat poured off him. His head was beaded with the stuff, big wet patches at his armpits. Thick veins stood out on his arms where he gripped the phone. Almost threw it through the window. Forced himself to place it back in its cradle.

The copper had finally got back to him with some intel. Stevie had to put two and two together, but he knew now. Worked out who'd been stitching him up all this time. If he was being honest with himself, he'd counted to three and a half, rather than four, but he put his minor doubts aside. Ultimately it *felt* right.

Harry Piles was a dead man. He just didn't know it yet.

Prison Break

Mr Lamb exits. It's surprisingly anti-climactic.

Gate opens.

Grey haired, well-dressed, entirely unremarkable man steps through.

Gate closes.

No clang of metal on metal, no sigh of release, no Edvard Munch screaming for a life lost.

Lucy and I had had to wait whilst Mr Lamb was inside. Said something about not being on the approved visitors list, or similar bollocks. It is dull. Lucy barely speaks, preoccupied with something she refuses to discuss, despite my repeated probing. Eventually, I give up and we spend the rest of the time in stony silence. Thank Christ he's back.

Mr Lamb puts a black gym bag into the boot, slides into the car, starts the engine and pulls away. He's making no effort to explain himself, so I ask, "What the fuck was that all about?"

"I met someone I used to work for. A finance expert," he says.

"Must be the only banker in recent history to be banged up."

He gives me a thin smile. "Ian Culpepper. You may have heard of him."

I shrug. Not particularly interested. "And?"

"He's been very helpful in our investigation."

I wait for more, but clearly that's it. I look over my shoulder at Lucy. She lifts an eyebrow in disinterest, then stares out of the window.

"Great."

Silence for an hour.

We draw up outside a shabby line of terraced houses. I stretch. I ache all over. The sign of a long day which comprised a kicking, a near death experience, hours in a car driving and hours waiting.

I've had better days, but I've also had many worse.

"I thought you said we'd be safer here," I say, peering at some dodgy-looking geezers down the road. They look suspiciously like they're inhaling something volatile from a plastic bag.

"You will," Mr Lamb says.

I say, still prissy, "I'll need to collect the Shit Machine."

"Pardon?"

Lucy says, "It's his knackered old car."

I'm all offended. "The Machine and I have been through a lot together. It's a reflection of my life to date."

We sit in silence for a moment. No-one quite knows what to say. I can hear the engine tick. At least the glue sniffers are moving off.

"All right, if it means that much to you, I'll go and collect it," Mr Lamb says. "You can't be seen around the guest house again."

"Thanks." I'm reluctant, but don't see much alternative.

He gets out, we follow. Places an entry card against a graffitied gate. There's a click, Mr Lamb pushes at the barrier, we enter a side alley. It's enclosed, dark, damp. Dogs bark. He pays them no attention.

A door at the far end. Heavy, thick, gleaming paintwork. He raps out a tattoo on the wood, waits a moment and unlocks this one. Then we're into a hallway. Empty except for a couple of CCTV monitors.

And a gun. Pointing at my head, millimetres from my left eye. The barrel looks huge. I can smell oil. And coffee. My heart rate skyrockets.

Mr Lamb pushes the weapon away, says, "Konstantin Boryakov, meet David Brodie."

Konstantin transfers the weapon to his left hand. It's tiny in his palm. He offers me his right to shake. The grip is tight, absolutely what I expect.

I look him up and down. Mostly up. And a fair bit of across. He's huge.

"Good meet you," he says. An accent as strong as his clasp. Eastern European. "I Russian," he says, anticipating the question on my lips. "KGB and FSB."

"KGB? What the fuck are you doing here?"

I laugh. He doesn't. I stop. Doesn't help slow my pulse.

"Long, dark story," he says. In an instant, his face transforms, any irritation brushed off his face. Booms, "Who this pretty lady?"

I begin to wonder if he's bi-polar. There's a Jekyll and Hyde behaviour about him.

"I'm Lucy Ryan," she says, offers a hand.

"No shaking! Kiss only!"

And he does, first one cheek, then the other. He has to lean down to do so. Lucy looks taken aback. As Konstantin withdraws, he spots the bullet wound, lifts her hair up and inspects it. She doesn't flinch.

"Nasty. Come, have something that help." Konstantin crooks a finger. No-one's arguing with the big bastard.

He leads us into the living room. It's functional, clean and white. Several comfortable armchairs and a coffee table are pretty much it for furniture. Some Russian icons and gaudy religious paintings on the wall, bars on the window, huge television in the corner.

"Sit," Konstantin says. "I make more coffee."

Which sounds like a great plan.

"Christ! What is this stuff?" I shudder. The coffee is like river mud. Although not as tasty.

"You no like?"

Konstantin is clearly not someone to deliberately upset, particularly when he has a gun to hand.

So I lie, say, "It's great!"

The Russian laughs, looks at Mr Lamb. "He bullshitter."

"What do you expect from a reporter?"

Konstantin barks out a laugh. Then scoops out some evil smelling lotion from a pot and holds it up for examination. Lucy's perched on the edge of a chair, waiting in less than anticipation by the look on her face.

"This from Japan," he says. "Herbal remedy. Will take pain away, accelerate healing process. Okay?"

She nods, closes her eyes. Konstantin liberally applies the cream. Lucy's trepidation transforms. A tickle of a smile crosses her lips. She murmurs, "That does feel good."

I feel a tiny pang of jealousy at the tenderness she's being shown by the Russian caveman. A Stone Age emotion stirs within me.

"Do you mind?" I ask, stick out a hand for the cream.

Part of my conscious mind (I hesitate to call it intelligence) screams at me: *'What the fuck are you doing?'*

Konstantin pauses, looks up, holds my gaze. He stands, towers over me, blocking out the light from the window. Presses the pot into my palm, gives me a slow wink. I breathe again. I take the Russian's place.

Lucy closes her eyes again, a bigger smile on her face.

"Huh," says Konstantin. "A reporter with feelings. May be hope for us yet."

Fire and Brimstone

Oakhill took in a lungful of air, huffed a tremendous sigh. "I'll say it one more time. I want them both dead. Now. One's a liability, the other's a serial fuck-up and a grass."

"A grass? What are you on about boss?"

"The mole. It's Piles."

Frank was utterly nonplussed.

"Since when?"

"Makes sense. He's a cop."

"Years ago, boss. He got banged up for taking bribes, remember?"

"Yeah, but once a cop, always a cop."

Frank wondered why Stevie had never said this before. However, he held his tongue. The turn of events suited him. Suspected he knew whose work this had been.

"Anyway, I've had some inside information that confirms it."

Frank swore internally. The copper. And he hadn't tipped off Frank. Decided not to argue the logic anymore. Besides, it suited him. Diverted Stevie's attention elsewhere.

"You're right boss. We can't have a grass in the ranks. I'll get it done. Any particular preference on method?"

Stevie looked at the devil tattoo on his left arm. Remembered simpler days, but said, "Fire and brimstone."

"Fire I can do. I've no fucking idea where to get brimstone."

Stevie glared at Frank. He left, calling for wood, petrol, and lots of matches.

Mr Lamb found the Shit Machine. It wasn't difficult. It stuck out like the proverbial sore thumb. It was barely a car. He wondered why the reporter had such an attachment to it. Spent five minutes searching the bodywork, what was left unravaged by rust, that is. Found nothing, no hidden secrets.

Mr Lamb shook his head. It must simply be an emotional attachment then. It was a piece of metal, no more, no less.

Mentally shrugged. The Shit Machine started first time. Mr Lamb wondered what all the fuss was about.

It was dark, not quite pitch black. A thin moon made fuck-all difference to the ambience. Frank, leant against a tree, sucked hard on the filter, drawing smoke-borne nicotine deep into his tar stricken lungs. The tip burnt orange, dimmed. He held the fumes in a moment, then they flared out of his nostrils, dragon-like. He lit another from the stub, discarded the dead one at his feet, where several already lay.

His men worked steadily, quietly. Stacking kindling, ramming rods of iron under the door handles, dousing the wood and the walls of the house with petrol. The noxious fumes hung heavy in the air.

"We're done," Squirrel said.

"About fucking time," he growled. "Thought you'd take so long, they'd wake up and walk out of there."

Frank received a low laugh in response.

"It wasn't a joke."

"Sorry," Squirrel mumbled.

"Fuck this, let's get it finished."

"Shouldn't we ...?"

"No warnings. We've been told to kill them both. So that's what we'll do."

Frank saw Squirrel's silhouette head shake. "It doesn't feel right, boss."

"What?" Frank asked, although he knew the answer.

"Piles. Yeah, he was a useless tub of lard, but a snitch? I don't believe it."

Frank shrugged. "And?"

"Nothing, I'm just saying, is all."

"Keep asking questions of the boss and you'll be in there with them, Squirrel. Do you want that?"

"No."

"Then he was a grass, get over it."

"Okay."

"Good. And if anyone manages to escape, shoot them and throw the body back into the flames."

"You got it, boss."

"Squirrel?"
"Yeah, boss?"
"Don't screw it up."
"I won't."

Gordon Dredge watched the men scurrying around below. He was an insomniac these days, but it looked like he had a long rest just ahead of him. Surprised to find he wasn't scared of death, now it was imminent. Dredge had nothing to love in this world, no-one to love him. Perhaps there was a better place ahead.

But probably not.

He sat down on the end of the bed. Harry Piles snored softly. Dredge wondered whether to wake him. Before the end came...

It took surprisingly little to get the fire going. The construction was timber-framed, built from ancient materials, tinder dry. That and the tanker's worth of fuel spread around the immediate area.

As always, it started small. Just the flick of a lighter. No-one made a sound. Frank could hear the little wheel grind on the flint from where he stood, saw the sparks.

In moments angry yellow flames flared upwards. The fire immediately took on a life of its own. It talked to them, growled, roared, shouted as if delighted to be set free to wreak havoc. Frank's men stepped backwards. Even he felt a little awed by its power. Unstoppable now.

He watched fingers creep up and around the old house, touching everything in its path. Like a paedophile.

Squirrel lit a petrol bomb, tossed it before the flammable fluid within caught and turned him into a human torch. Crashed through a window. Within moments, four more followed into various parts of the house. They burst and fire leapt up inside as well as out.

Frank saw a shadow move across a bedroom window. It popped open. One of his men fired a shot. The shape disappeared. It had looked like Piles. He would be shitting himself. Frank knew it wouldn't be long before the screaming started. He'd heard it plenty of times before. High pitched, shrill. He imagined it would be excruciatingly painful, burning alive. Feeling your hair burn, your skin crisp, your fat boil. It never lasted for long. He'd bet Dredge would give in to the fear. His bullshit, stiff upper lip façade would splinter ...

Night had turned into day. Dredge could feel the heat on the soles of his feet, the sweat running down his face, his body soaked with perspiration. But what struck him most was the noise. It was incredible. Like the sound came straight out of the depths of Hell, a myriad of tortured souls unleashed temporarily.

Not even Piles could sleep through it. Dredge watched him slowly come around, sit up in bed, gradually focus.

"What's going on, old man?" Piles said, torpor lying heavily on his words. "What you doing in my room?"

"We're being murdered."

Piles barked out his usual derisive laugh. But the sound was strangled off as he caught sight of the flames. The big man stumbled to the window, looked out.

"What the fuck?" Piles shouted. "This isn't right! They'll want you, not me!" He pushed open a window.

There was gunfire. Piles ducked back in pure reflex. He turned to Dredge, realisation on his open-mouthed features.

"Probably best to let them shoot you, Harry. Get it over quickly."

When Piles spoke, his voice was barely a whisper, hard to catch over the flames. "I don't want to die, Gordon."

"I know, my boy. I know," Dredge said. He stood up and enveloped Harry in his arms. "But it comes to us all one day."

He smelt the body odour, heard the smothered sob, then felt Piles return the hug, bury his head into Dredge's shoulder. The pair stood like that for a moment before a lurch, a roar and ...

Blackness ...

There was a clatter, like popcorn, only one or two at first, but then too many to be counted. Frank knew it was the tiles going.

Moments later, there was a drawn-out groan and the roof cascaded in. A burst of sparks rose high into the sky, as if it were a Guy Fawkes bonfire.

"No-one's getting out of there alive," he said. "Let's go before the law arrives."

The Merc and van was a mile down the road when the first of eight fire engines raced past in the opposite direction, blue lights flashing.

Frank looked back, saw a pall of grey smoke billowing, smiled to himself. A job well done. It was a pity about Piles. He'd had nothing against the man, other than him being an ex-copper, but luck had to be capitalised on. And fuck-ups were fuck-ups.

Steroid Stevie would be very pleased with him. And, for now, that was all that mattered.

They reached the rendezvous point, an out-of-the-way car park in the middle of a wood usually frequented by walkers and twitchers. The group split up into separate vehicles, took the evidence with them.

As his men drove away, Frank, alone now in the Merc, pulled out his phone. Called Stevie, said, "Yeah, it's done, boss. You'll see it on the news soon."

"Nice one, Frank. Knew I could count on you. Take the boys out, get them pissed. On me."

"Thanks, boss. Will do."

He disconnected, tapped out a text, smiled like a barracuda.

Up here on the car park roof it was windy. The smell of the sea was strong, the air tasted salty after the smog of the city.

The copper confirmed the line of sight. No problems.

Checked the wiring. All safe and sound.

A brief squawk of electronic signal and the explosives would do what they were supposed to do.

Kill people.

Made sure the parking ticket was evident in the window, twenty four hours paid for. More than enough.

Just a little more time, then freedom forever. If a few innocent bystanders got caught in the blast, so be it.

The copper closed the boot. The bang was loud in the silence.

It would be louder tomorrow.

Ashes To Ashes

Yesterday

I see it on the news. Well, actually Konstantin hears about it on the radio first. He shouts for us to come into the living room, flicks on the television, waits for the ticker tape headlines, points when the relevant item appears.

I can't believe what I'm reading and flop down into a chair, lean forward with my arms on my thighs.

Lucy wanders in with Mr Lamb. She stands beside me, idly rests a hand on my shoulder. I feel ice through my shirt. She looks distracted, doesn't seem to focus on the screen. My tiredness is suddenly gone. I barely slept a wink last night. Partially due to the pain in my finger, but mostly thinking about Lucy.

Mr Lamb drops a set of car keys into my palm, but I barely register them because all my attention is on the screen. There's total silence, except for the newsreader's serious tones as she talks to a security expert about the latest problem in the Middle East.

"Fuck. I wonder if he's okay?" Lucy says.

"No idea, yet," I reply.

Then the presenter finally announces a catastrophic fire at Dredge's house. Everyone seems to tilt closer as the shot switches to an overhead of some smouldering ruins in the grey dawn. Fire engines and police cars are scattered haphazardly around the periphery.

It looks like a child's play scene.

The place is entirely gutted. It's impossible to reconcile the shape of tumbled walls with my memory. The camera zooms in briefly, shows some bricks here, scorched struts there and a couple of pieces of blackened masonry that will have to be torn down eventually, even though they've outlasted the fire.

Then the scene becomes a white tent in the middle of the ruin, a stark contrast to the charred backdrop. It's an easy assumption to make that a corpse lies underneath.

I hadn't liked Gordon Dredge. He'd been one of life's takers, and he'd totally screwed mine up, but I don't think he or anyone else should die like this. It must have been a horrible experience.

The Russian breaks the silence, says, "Big problem. Witness gone."

"This wasn't ever going to court, Konstantin," Mr Lamb says.

"So, what next?" I ask. I'm feeling a bit lost.

"We can't sit around waiting for something to happen," Mr Lamb says. "The only thing I can think of is to investigate the fire."

He pulls his driving gloves on.

"I'm going with you," I say.

"Me too," chips in Lucy.

Mr Lamb shakes his head. "We're not going in mob-handed. You can come along, David, but, Lucy, you're staying with Konstantin."

She looks pissed. The Russian looks delighted.

Once we arrive at Dredge's house, it's my turn to be annoyed. I'm not allowed across the police cordon, so I get to sit in Lamb's hire car.

Again.

I play a few games on my phone to pass the time whilst my new friend gets to do the interesting stuff.

Double-Cross

Frank waited for the connection to be made, listened to the insistent ringing. The call went to voicemail. He rang again, three times. His irritation rose with each missed opportunity. He had news and was desperate to deliver it.

Stevie finally picked up. His voice sounded thick with sleep. He said, "What the fuck do you want, Frank? Have you any idea what time it is?"

"We were attacked, boss."

"What you on about? Are you pissed?"

Frank explained, then said, "All of 'em, boss. All dead. I think it was them Chechens. Must have been."

"Four men! Fuckin' four men dead. Four fuckin' men dead, for fuck's sake."

Frank didn't reply, could hear Stevie breathing a little more steadily now down the line.

"Two questions. Why didn't you call me straight away?"

"There was no way I was leaving the bodies lying around. I got 'em cleared up. Took a bit of time."

"Okay, good thinking. Second question. Why ain't you the late, Frank McGowan?"

"Dunno, Stevie. Right place, wrong time, I guess."

"Tell me again what happened. This time very … fucking … slowly."

So Frank did:

We'd been out on the piss all night, tearing up the town – me, Squirrel, Barnie, Tyrone and Jimmy. Eyeing up the birds, throwing back the pints, twatting the ... twats. Been a great laugh. One of the best. You'd have loved it.

Ok, I'll get to the point.

Sorry.

As we walked back to the car, arguing about who was the most drunk and therefore the designated driver, it happened.

Two men stepped out from an alley. We paid them no attention. No-one would dare pick a fight with us.

Until we heard the unmistakable 'snick' of a hammer being pulled back. The laughter stopped immediately then, I can tell you, Stevie.

Two men. Two sawn-offs.

Four cartridges. No time for last words.

Triggers pulled, great flames erupted from the end of the barrels. And a shitload of buckshot.

Jimmy and Squirrel were cut nearly in two, died instantly.

Barnie and Tyrone caught most of the rest. They were probably alive when they hit the road, but the killers pulled out pistols.

I ran then.

Ran like fuck as the pair put bullets into Barnie and Tyrone.

Double-taps, quick as you like. Head and heart. Belt and braces.

"And you weren't hit?" Stevie asked. Frank could hear the incredulity in his voice. He was breathing heavily down the line.

Like he'd been running too.

Or was getting a blow job.

"Cut on the face by something. Piece of masonry, maybe. Thrown up by a bullet that hit the wall when they shot at me. I was lucky, boss."

"Luckiest fucker in history, Frank."

"Don't feel like it. Can you send someone to pick me up? I don't wanna be seen walking around with someone else's blood all over me."

"Where are you?"

Frank told him, disconnected the call, smiled to himself. Tapped out a quick text, "Sorted."

Deleted it immediately.

He couldn't quite believe they'd got away with it.

Most of the story had been true.

Frank had hung back a couple of yards, let the lads get well in front of him. They were all pissed as arseholes.

But not Frank, he'd reigned in on the drink. Acted smashed, been stone-cold sober. Could hold his alcohol better than the next man.

So the boys were ahead as the copper stepped out the mouth of the alley, joined Frank, slapped a shotgun into his palm, metal warm to the touch. Like it was alive. He cocked the brutal weapon, relished the noise it made. Small, but huge.

Loved the way the boys stop dead in their tracks. In a moment, that analogy would literally be true. But for now, they turned around.

They laughed, thinking it a joke. Missed the dark glint in his eye, Frank's eye. Told him to stop fucking around, laughed some more.

Until Frank pulled the trigger, hammer dropped, ignited the projectiles.

Deafening roar. Blood and flesh flew, spattered Frank. He didn't even blink.

Out came the handgun. Double-tap from the copper to finish off the two that were still moving. No witnesses. A couple more into the pair cut in half by the buckshot trail.

For appearance. The work of moments to accomplish.

Then Frank reluctantly passed back the shotgun. Thought first about using it on the copper, but knew he had no shells.

He and the copper stuffed the bodies into the car boot, melted away into the darkness well before the sirens started.

Four men down. The perfect end to a great night.

The plan was coming together beautifully. Blaming the Chechens was just brilliant. His idea.

What fucking genius.

Mr Lamb had to show his fake identification to gain access to the cordoned-off crime scene.

First, general impressions. Nothing had been left untouched by the vicious conflagration. Puddles everywhere, the ground soaked from the thousands of gallons of water that had been used to douse the fire. Nevertheless, plumes of smoke still rose here and there.

The great house was a charred skeleton, the contents turned into twisted lumps of metal, plastic – and bone.

Second, determine the cause.

He tracked down a fire officer, flashed his ID again. The man looked tired, harassed, a smudge of ash across his face.

"By the time the shout went out and the Brigade arrived, the fire had taken a complete hold," he explained. "There wasn't anything the boys could do to stop it." He shrugged to emphasise the inevitability of the disaster.

"Any idea how it started?" Mr Lamb asked.

"Just sniff the air, mate. That'll tell you. Sorry, gotta go."

Mr Lamb knew what a fire needed to exist – fuel, oxygen, energy.

He drew a breath in through his nose, a process he'd so far avoided.

Incredibly, the bouquet of petrol was detectable over the stench of ash and death – that was the former provided for. The oxygen was, of course, naturally present in the air. The energy would be the heat of the fire itself.

Third, find the bodies.

He headed towards one of the white-suited fire investigators already picking their way through the site. The man was on his knees, examining something unseen on the ground. Mr Lamb tapped him on his shoulder.

The investigator jerked, focus broken. He glared but stood up, pulled a mask down off his mouth which mimicked the displeasure in his eyes. He didn't peel off a glove to shake Mr Lamb's hand. The demeanour was clearly, 'I'm busy, leave me alone.'

A flash of ID brought a sigh and a hint of acceptance to his twisted features.

"It'll take days to properly investigate," he explained without Mr Lamb needing to ask. "We'll have to peel back the debris layers, see what we can find, then issue a full report."

"I'd just like your initial impression please. Then I'll leave you to your task."

The investigator grumbled again. Mr Lamb remained impassive, let the wave of the man's frustration break over him.

"Okay, if it means you'll let me get back to my work." Another sigh. "We've found multiple seats of fire. By that I mean the origin of where it started, of course. Because there are so many of them, it adds to my initial suspicion of arson. I think they used petrol, it's the most likely, but I'll have to confirm with hydrocarbon sniffers."

"No discarded containers?" Mr Lamb asked.

The investigator shook his head. "None immediately obvious."

Careful people then. Professionals. Or at the least, knowledgeable of police procedures.

"And the bodies?"

"Yes, two. Not pleasant to observe. It's entirely possible to find a corpse intact. It takes hours at elevated temperatures to destroy a body entirely. Most people don't appreciate that."

Mr Lamb did, but he said, "Thank you, most helpful." The investigator nodded, pulled his mask up and knelt down.

As he beat a retreat to the car, Mr Lamb experienced a tiny twinge of regret for Dredge. Not because he'd liked the man, far from it, but there was information he hadn't been able to transfer over.

Disappointing, but perhaps not disastrous.

Power, Corruption And Lies

Mr Lamb returns to the car. I stop playing snake, pretend to look serious. He slides inside. Then his phone rings.

"Hello?" he says. "Yes, hold on a moment."

Takes the phone away from his ear, presses the speaker key, puts a finger to his lips. He wants silence from me. Not my forte.

"Hello? Hello? Mr Lamb are you still there?" says a reedy voice, continues before his question is answered. "It's Governor Field."

"Yes, I know. Sorry, I lost you briefly. Bad reception around here."

I can see five bars on the mobile. Full signal strength. I raise an eyebrow, he shrugs.

"Ah, modern technology, eh?"

"Seems so. How can I help you, Governor?"

"I've some rather sad news I'm afraid. I regret to tell you that Ian Culpepper has expired."

Mr Lamb looks at me. He seems surprised, but takes the news in his stride. Voice bereft of emotion, he says, "Somewhat unexpected."

"Yes. Very unfortunate."

"Can I enquire as to the cause of death?"

"Asphyxiation brought on by dangling himself from a rope whilst not having his feet in contact with the floor."

"So, hanging?"

"Yes. That."

"Any suspicious circumstances?"

"No, of course not! We believe suicide brought on by depression."

"Did he receive any visitors in the time since my last visit?"

"Er, let me check." We heard the rustle of paper.

"No, no, there doesn't appear to have been anyone."

"Are you certain?"

"I think so."

"Because yesterday you said I was being treated as a priority over someone else."

"Ah, yes. So I did."

Mr Lamb waited, let the silence stretch. Eventually, Field filled it, said, "I'm not allowed to tell you."

"Okay, Governor. You need to make a decision here."

"I'm sorry?"

"Who you're more scared of. Me or the other person?"

Field stutters, tells us who. Mr Lamb ends the call. We stare at each other.

"So you take some financial information to your expert and now he's dead."

"Yes."

"What did he tell you?"

"The usual. Corruption and lies. He showed me a partial bank account number and told me that if I completed it, I'd have my suspect."

"I may be able to help there."

Hold up the USB stick.

For the first time, I see Mr Lamb smile.

Wright Time

The phone on Stevie's desk jangled. He leaned forward, picked it up, growled, "Yeah?"

There was an awful pause as Stevie listened. He sat back heavily, took in some more. Shock turned to anger.

Frank tried very hard to fix a puzzled expression on his face, even though he knew exactly what was going on.

"Get them out on fucking bail now! No, don't give me a single reason *why* it can't be done. Make it *happen*."

Stevie slammed the phone down in its cradle. Over steepled fingers, Oakhill fixed Frank with a venomous look. Then again, Stevie only did venomous or asleep.

"What's going on, boss?" Frank finally asked.

"A couple of the boys have been lifted."

"Fuck."

"Couldn't have said it better myself, Frank. That was the legal eagle on the phone. That clever bastard I keep on the payroll. Wright by name, right by nature."

"Boss, you said a couple of the boys were nicked?"

"Yeah, bit distracted, Frank. Fuck's sake."

Stevie ran a hand over his bald head. Frank was pleased to see some perspiration there.

"Go on, boss."

"Wrightie told me they're suspects in the little blaze that accidentally destroyed Dredge's house."

"Oh shit."

"As you heard, I want them out, but that might be a bit of a problem. Some evidence or something that ties them directly to the bleeding thing."

"How did that happen?"

"You tell me. You were there!" Stevie's glare intensified. Frank maintained eye contact, although he was desperate to look away.

"Nah, this doesn't make sense. We cleared up afterwards. I checked."

"Then someone screwed up because, apparently, the lads were stopped and had a couple of jerry cans in the boot. Mr Wright says they've been placed at the scene via some footprints."

"That's just shit luck, Stevie."

"The only bit of fortune was they were driving their own cars, not one of mine. Otherwise the cops would be all over my back. I just hope the lawyer can do something about it. He's got us out of a few shitty situations in the past."

"I don't know what to say, boss."

"Me neither. Get the fuck out of here so I can think about what to do with you."

Frank closed the door behind him. He wasn't scared by Stevie's threats. One of the benefits of the gang shrinking – those that were left became more critical.

Lock and Load

The copper was ready.

Five balls to set rolling.

Concentrate on the first three. Once done, hit the last two.

One: The Terrorists.

The copper gave the Chechens an address, sent over two photographs.

Two: The Insider.

He tapped in a text, said, "Have to meet. Situation critical." And a location.

Three: The Target.

Made a call to Stevie and informed on his informer.

The Terrorists.

Adam opened the e-mail, didn't recognise the address. Why would he? But one of the faces burned into his memory forever. Would be even after his death. Turned the laptop around, showed Ilyas, watched his eyes narrow.

"I'll get the men," Ilyas said.

Adam's hands shook with emotion.

At last, he thought.

The Insider.

Stole a quick glance at the time. The rendezvous could just about be made. Running shoes would be required though.

Banged out a reply, made excuses, got moving.

The Target.

Stevie left the house with his bodyguards, slid into the back seat, sat back and avoided thinking of the potential consequences. It was shit or bust now.

The Terrorists.

Two cars and a van pulled up into the narrow alley. The latter was loaded.

Semi-automatic machine guns, handguns and a shitload of ammo.

Adam tooled himself up, ready to go. A Makarov in hand, another stuffed in his waistband.

He wasn't taking any chances.

Split the men into two teams.

Five through the front, three more at the rear with Ilyas.

Adam texted the copper. Said, "We're going in."

The Insider.
Arrived at the meeting point, glanced up and down the street.

Nothing obviously out of place.

But something felt wrong.

The copper wasn't here.

And instinct.

The Target.
"We've been made," Stevie said.

He watched the informer through binoculars, studied the face, what expressions skittered across.

None at all.

Which wasn't right.

The driver turned the key, ready to fire up the engine for a quick getaway.

The Terrorists.
One of Adam's men laughed, "It will be like shooting fish in a fucking barrel."

"No. It will not," Adam said. "They are not the old men they seem. They are dangerous. They are deadly."

"But they bleed like the next man," Ilyas said.

Based on experience, Adam wasn't so sure about that.

The Insider.
When it happened, there was nothing could be done to avoid it. No amount of practice really prepares you.

All the capture training?

You know in your heart at the time it's colleagues grabbing you.

Not the bad guys.

Then someone points a gun at you, you're in the boot of a car and realise not even Houdini could get himself out of this mess.

Kicked, screamed. No-one to hear or care.

The Target.
Stevie sent the copper a text. Said, "Got it."

The copper got the results one after the other, laughed. Next.
Four: The Patsy.
Called, told him where to be. Said this was it.
Five: The Reporter.
Sent a text, said, "If you survive, ring this number."

The Patsy.
Frank thought the copper's suggestion as to where it would go down was a fitting one. An excellent location for Stevie to hand over his empire.

And for the copper to die.

The Reporter.
David Brodie felt his phone vibrate and pulled out his phone.

The copper grinned, put an eye to the scope, could see the roof perfectly, had a wonderful wide view.

The copper was already a hell of a lot richer.

Soon be free to actually spend it.

Panic Room

I receive a text, don't understand it. I'm about to raise the puzzle with Mr Lamb when there's a heavy thud, followed by another. The building shudders slightly, like a boxer taking a punch.

Mr Lamb's head goes up. Alert. Hackles up. Primed.

"Armed men!" Konstantin shouts from the hallway.

We run through. The Russian points at the monitors. One shows the front door being shoulder-barged by two figures whilst colleagues peer into the windows. But, remember, they're frosted and barred.

I hear barking, screams and two shots. Quick taps. Then another report, a couple of seconds later. No more canine clamour.

"Glock, Makarov," Konstantin said. Mr Lamb agreed. Neither mentions the animals that must be dead.

More men then appear on the screen that displays the rear of the house. One is limping, an arm hanging low. They start to kick at the door.

"How long will it take them to break it down?" I ask.

Konstantin shrugs. "Depends. Like that? Thirty minutes."

As if they're psychic, the physical abuse being doled out to the resisting entrance dies away. Two people move out of sight. Within a minute they return, begin to fix what looks like plasticine around the door handle.

"And if they have explosives?"

"Half a second." Konstantin grimaces.

"Then we'd better move," Mr Lamb says.

The Russian pulls a grey card out of his pocket, holds it against the wall to the right of the monitors. An entrance clicks open where before there hadn't been one. He flings it back dramatically.

"After you," he says.

I pause to look. A bare bulb overhead shows stairs descending.

"Go!" the Russian urges. I skittle down, heavy feet following me. I hear the flap snap shut above.

Twenty odd steps and I'm in a small opening. White walls encompass me, the space clearly cut out of the rock. I can see chisel marks in the chalk, bits of flint sticking out here and there.

Ahead is a big, fuck-off steel door and a keypad to the right. Mr Lamb is on my heels, Konstantin a couple of paces to the rear. He pushes past me, taps in a code, presses on the door. It swings back soundlessly.

My jaw drops.

Konstantin shoves me inside and the three inch thick metal slab cuts us off from above.

"Fuck me," I breathe. I've never seen anything like it. "Is this a panic room?"

"For us, no. For them, yes," Konstantin says.

We're in a small cube-shaped space. Two more monitors on the wall reveal the interior of the house. But that's not what's got my attention.

It's the rack upon rack of firearms and ammunition.

Handguns, machine guns, shotguns, sniper rifles. I swear there's a rocket launcher too. Green boxes on the floor with 'Explosives' stencilled on the side. Konstantin goes to the framework, starts pulling weapons down and placing them on the small table in the centre of the space. It's like something from Grand Theft Auto.

There's a double BOOM above. The monitor screen shows debris burst into the hallway, followed more sedately by a dust cloud through which men run in, guns nestled into their shoulders. They scan around, in and out of rooms. Laser beams flash.

They'll be here in moments.

Take The High Road

Ilyas led seven combatants through the house, guns raised, one left outside in reserve.

He entered the final room. A couple of chairs and a table. Empty of human form.

"Clear!" he shouted.

They must be upstairs.

The high ground. Fine when you occupy it. Crap when you don't. Worse when you have to assault it.

The stairs were steep, narrow. They cut back on themselves halfway up in a dogleg. Difficult to see what was up there without sticking your head round the corner. And probably getting it shot off.

"Take a look," Ilyas barked.

None stepped forward. Ilyas grabbed the one with the limp, trousers soaked in blood that seeped out of the multiple punctures the dog's razor-sharp teeth had produced, threw him to the bottom of the stairs.

No bullets.

A temporary survival. Ilyas would probably shoot him later anyway. For being so careless.

"They're probably cowering in one of the bedrooms. We'll storm the stairs, kick the rooms in one at a time."

With Ilyas at point, they did just that. Boots thumped, they ran up as one. Got to the top safely.

Doors all closed. Ilyas pointed to the first. A pair to either side, one to kick, one to shove a gun barrel in, shoot.

Crashed open. Bullets sprayed. Ilyas glanced inside. Bed, carpet, wardrobe that looked like they'd been attacked by giant moths. Otherwise empty.

Three more rooms, lots more bullets, all curiously vacant. Bathroom, no-one hiding behind the curtain.

"Doesn't make any sense," said Ilyas.

Crossfire

"Amateurs," Konstantin says. He seems genuinely affronted by the enemy's method.

The Russian passes me a handgun. I couldn't tell you what the make is. It's big, heavy, shiny, but fits snugly into my palm. Like it's been there forever. It makes me feel giddy with power, yet shit scared at the same time.

"Know how shoot?" Konstantin asks.

I shake my head. It's spinning. Everything has taken such a rapid turn. Yet, with all the chaos above, the atmosphere in the panic room is anything but. It's utter calm. Like they've got their game heads on, in the zone, before the big match.

Konstantin takes it back. "Safety here," he says, pointing. "On, no bullets. Off, aim big barrel at man, squeeze trigger. Slowly. Big bang, man fall down dead. Easy."

"Okay, sounds it. Thanks." I'm lying, by the way.

Mr Lamb is tooled up as well. A shotgun, barrel wickedly short, plus a revolver in his waistband, several magazines and a handful of shells in his pockets. Jacket discarded on the table. I guess he doesn't want it to catch on any snags. His pupils are enlarged, almost totally black. He's always scared the shit out of me but now he's armed?

Terrifying.

"Ready?" Konstantin asks. He's a machine gun and a couple of pistols holstered at each hip. Along with what look like grenades on a belt.

Mr Lamb rolls his eyes at the Russian. "Overkill," he says.

"Da. That the point, is not?"

"Are we going up?" I ask.

Konstantin answers my question by pulling on one of the weapons shelves. Behind it is a dark hole. He smiles murderously at me.

The tunnel is cold, clammy. Water drips on my head. It's dimly lit by bulbs periodically fixed to the wall. Konstantin leads. I'm in the middle. Mr Lamb to the rear. A very unsavoury sandwich.

The walk is mercifully brief. I don't like enclosed spaces. Then we start to rise. Hit some steep steps. At the top is an egress, bolted from the inside. More monitors. They show the hall empty, but the landing full.

Konstantin whispers, "Spread out to rooms, one each. Wait for idiots to come down. When I give signal, cover ears, close eyes."

"Why?" I say.

The Russian taps one of the canisters on his hip. "Flash Bang. Very bright, very loud. No peeking."

"Okay."

"Then start shooting," Konstantin says. He grins even wider.

The Russian slides the locks back. They're well oiled, silent.

He indicates to flick safety to OFF, pushes at the door. It opens into a war zone full of wood, dust, plaster. The air has cleared at least. Primarily due to the amount of ventilation created by the large holes front and back, where the entrances had been.

Large splinters are embedded in the wall, the whole area is shredded. Anyone caught in here when the explosives detonated would have been slaughtered. A click and the entrance to the tunnel is shut off.

Konstantin goes to the living room, stepping carefully over the debris. The stairs are behind him now. Mr Lamb to the dining room. My post is the kitchen, at the end of the corridor by the cellar.

Between us, we've a killing field.

I can hear voices. They float down from above. Lots of swearing, a language I don't recognise. I try and still my breathing. It's so loud, they must be able to hear me. My heart pulses in my chest, battering my ribcage at an unhealthy rate – my metabolism's way off the chart.

The stairs creak. They're coming down. Mr Lamb winks at me. He looks like he's enjoying himself. Me? I bet I'm as white as a sheet.

I check the safety. It's set to off. Definitely. Check it again. Yep. Off.

There's a load of guys congregating in the hallway. I count eight. They look to the grey-haired leader. I recognise him,

Adam's gun-toting friend. I suddenly see them as sheep wanting to be herded, but in reality for the slaughter.

Then a silver canister springs out, lands at their feet. Heads twist, guns raise and swing. I turn away, jam my fingers hard in my ears, scrunch my eyes hard shut.

The BANG is deafening nevertheless.

My head rings. I may as well have not had my eyelids down, the flash is so bright, like looking at the sun through binoculars.

I can vaguely hear screams. Then gunshots. Automatic fire. Controlled bursts, multiples of three – gap – then three more shots in a repeat pattern. The heavy reports of a shotgun.

I turn back, raise my gun, poke it out from the jamb.

Sudden, total silence.

Bodies are heaped on top of each other, limbs skewed at crazy angles, as if they've been thrown up in the air to land in a jumble. No movement from a single one.

"Coming out!" Mr Lamb shouts. He steps into the hall, smoking shotgun barrel pointing at the corpses. Konstantin joins him in an identical pose.

There's a slight movement. Konstantin squats down, looks at the man. Grey covered with blood.

"Ilyas," Konstantin says. "Unpleasant to see you again."

He spits, unleashes a string of swear words. Konstantin shakes his head slightly, like a father disappointed in a young child. He stands up, shoots Ilyas in the head.

"Old enemy," Konstantin says, like that explains everything.

Adam's Apple

Adam had listened to the commotion with mounting confusion. The growling of the dogs, the two shots, all white noise. He idly glanced up and down the back alley, not really expecting any witnesses and confirmed this to be the case.

He'd masked his surprise when one of the guys returned to collect some Semtex. "Solid doors," was the explanation.

A minute later, twin crumps as the explosives were expended. Then … silence. He should have heard the staccato of gunfire, but nothing. The minutes stretched.

A massive crack. Then shooting, not wayward either. Short bursts, well controlled. The armament music accompanied by the deeper bass of a shotgun. Professionals.

Then it was over as soon as it had begun. Adam began running.

Blind Luck

I see movement at what was the front door. Dark hair, smudge of a face, gun. Konstantin turns. He won't be able to bring his weapon to bear in time.

I squeeze the trigger, loose off a shot but close my eyes at the last moment. Like when someone takes a photo and you blink.

When I look again, there's a chunk of plaster been blown off the wall at head height. He's gone. Konstantin is at the gap, fires a triple. He throws his machine gun down, yanks a revolver from a holster, dashes out.

Mr Lamb follows in his wake, drops the shotgun into the rubble, unlimbers a handgun too. My blood up, I put my head down and follow without a single thought.

Konstantin moves with surprising speed for such a large man, but Mr Lamb effortlessly keeps up with him. I'm way behind and losing ground all the time.

The shooter is rounding the corner of the terraced row. Konstantin fires a shot whilst in full flow.

The bark of a pistol in return, someone at the corner. I can see the flashes. Konstantin slows to a walk. He and Mr Lamb take opposite sides of the alley, exchange shots as they pace forward. One hits the mark, throws the guy backwards.

Konstantin takes off again. As he runs past the wounded man, he drops the muzzle, puts a couple of rounds in the guy. His body jerks. Mr Lamb, close behind, ignores the corpse.

Then they're out of sight.

Moments later, I hear more gunfire.

A Rapid Retreat

Adam's legs pumped furiously, propelled him at fast, this time away from the scene. Glad he'd been wise enough to sacrifice one of his men as a rear guard. Ducked when he heard a bullet whizz past his ear, felt the white hot heat.

He reached the car, leapt in, bent as low as possible whilst he started the ignition. The engine coughed into life. Threw the car into first gear, mashed the accelerator to the floor, pushed it into second when the engine whined like a torture victim.

The car bounced through potholes. Adam prayed a tyre wouldn't burst.

Several more shots, a couple of thuds into the bodywork somewhere. Rear window exploded, showered the interior with glass, passed through the front window. Left a small hole and a spider's web of cracks.

He swung the Glock over his shoulder, fired off a couple himself, although there was a tiny chance of him hitting anyone. Within seconds, he was away and out of sight.

Adam squeezed the brake, fighting the urge to keep racing, didn't want to bring any more attention to himself than he had to. Forced his jumping body to slow it down. He gritted his teeth a few times, like he was on speed. Knew he'd have to ditch the car, and soon.

The Chechen was desperately trying to hold it together. Internally, he raged, could feel his engorged veins pulsing. Heart butterflied, like his blood was marmalade, thick and lumpy.

He'd been lucky to make it out alive. All of his soldiers were dead, even Ilyas. Indestructible Ilyas. But many of his friends and comrades had died over the years. The latest were unfortunately just a few more on a very long list.

He pulled over in a dingy side street, turned the engine off, but left the keys in the ignition, got walking. With a bit of luck, someone would steal it soon.

Adam had a score to settle.

Just Another Gunfight

I finally round the corner. Konstantin and Mr Lamb are firing at a fast-receding black Audi. The back window bursts, a muzzle flash from inside, but the car speeds away and then is gone.

Konstantin mutters in Russian. I assume he's swearing.

"Who was that?" I ask.

"Ghosts from the past," Konstantin says, then glares at me.

I wonder what I've done wrong and ask.

"You save my life," he replies.

"Not really," I protest.

Fuck, if helping him elicits this response, I don't want to fall out with the guy.

"Da. I in your debt."

Then he envelopes me in a bear hug, feels like he's going to suffocate me. Some way of showing me gratitude. He steps back. "You ever need anything, just call."

I look at the pistol in my hand, say, "I'm sick of gunfights."

"Can never have too much of a good thing, as long as it bad guys getting shot," the Russian replies. Then he smiles. "Love shooting people."

He's a fucking maniac. But I can't help be drawn to him.

I remember the text then. Read it again, finally get a chance to show the screen to Mr Lamb.

"Extremely odd," he says. "Call the number, but put it on speaker."

I do. Get a robotic voice, can't tell if it's male or female. It says, "Congratulations Mr Brodie on making it through in one piece. Did your friends survive also?"

Mr Lamb touches my arm, shakes his head.

"No."

The robotic voice chuckles. "I suspect you are attempting to pull the wool over my eyes." Mr Lamb appears not to have registered the pun, his expression is impassive. "If you are alive, then so are they. Anyway, it doesn't matter. That was just a sideshow. You have some place to go."

"Do I?"

"Yes, aren't you missing someone?"

I remember. In all the chaos, I hadn't thought about it.

The voice tells me what to do.

Mr Lamb grabs my arm, arrests my dash.

"David, it's a trap!"

Of course it is. I know that already. Shrug. "I have to go."

"Yes, I know, but wait a moment. Let us help."

"Okay, I'll bring the car up front. Be ready."

Back round the corner and there's the Shit Machine. Nicely parked, perfectly against the kerb.

I yank at the door. For fuck's sake, locked. Ram the key into the hole, almost break it off. Twist it and a knob pops up inside. I don't think I've ever seen it do that. I didn't even know it had one.

Turn the engine over, twice, three times. It doesn't start. I need to be careful in case it floods and then I'll be screwed. Take a deep breath. Don't bother to say a prayer, as God is a fallacy, but I do ask for luck from somewhere, anywhere.

Flick the ignition one more time. Holy Mother and Mary, the Shit Machine starts.

"Thank you," I say to nobody.

I pull up in front of the house with a screech of brakes.

Mr Lamb is with Konstantin, who has a large black case in his left hand. They look like they're hanging around for a bus. The pair get in.

"Go," Mr Lamb says. "I'll tell you where to drop us off."

The Damned Unite

"Frank? We've a job on. We're on the way over."
"What is it, Stevie?"
"There's shit to settle. See you in five."

Frank disconnected, thought for a few minutes, eventually decided he should call the copper. It was answered immediately.
"Stevie's just rung. He's picking me up in a minute."
"Good. Everything gets settled today."
Frank heard a horn blow, said, "Gotta go."
But the copper had already disconnected.
He picked up his pistol, a six-shooter, put it into a shoulder holster. Waited for the elevator. Knew that Stevie would be swearing at the delay, made him smile.
"You took your fucking time," Stevie said as he slid into the BMW. Immediately, it pulled away from the kerb, Bob the driver not hanging around.
Frank shrugged. "Twelfth floor, boss. Can't do much about it." He heard a thud from behind. "Got someone in the boot?"
Stevie avoided the question, looked out the window. Frank noticed he had his sleeves rolled up, tats on view. Saw the devil on the left arm.
Like the old days.

Lost Girl

I stab at the buttons of my mobile, try to call Lucy again. It goes straight to voicemail. Where is the woman? I need to see her. Right now. To make sure she's okay.

"No answer?" Mr Lamb asks.

I shake my head.

"Not good sign," Konstantin says.

I glare at him in the rear-view mirror.

Accelerate harder.

The Beginning Of The End

Frank felt a bit sick by the time they reached the roof, all that going round and round. He didn't like multi-storeys. Grim shit-holes, usually. This one was no exception.

Bob parked up.

"Get out," Stevie said.

"Okay, boss. Anything else you need?"

"Just pass me the keys. Find your own way home."

Bob handed them over, slammed the door behind him. Frank ignored the driver's departure, kept his eyes on Stevie.

"How do you want to do this?" Frank asked. He had his pistol out, barrel a few feet away from Stevie's gut.

"What, are you expecting me to beg?" Oakhill said.

"Something like that, Stevie. Do you know how sick I am of taking your shit? Sucking up to you, having to do your crap, even when it's a stupid decision. All the time thinking you're so clever, when I'm behind your back, waiting with the knife."

"That's how it works, pal. One at the top, everyone underneath."

"Yeah? Well now it's me at the top."

"Really?"

It was then Frank started to reassess his situation. Stevie was unnaturally calm, totally in control, smiling even. He'd expected fireworks, a headlong charge maybe, or a bullet. But ... nothing.

"One last request, Frank?"

"Sure, fuck it, why not."

Stevie pulled out a phone, scrolled through a list, made a selection.

"Do you know who I'm calling?"

"Why would I care? It could be any one of your birds."

Then Frank could hear a faint ring tone. It sounded like it was coming from the boot.

Adam pulled into the garage, parked on the ground floor. Shut the door, looked for the stairs, saw them, pulled his gun out. Took the steps two at a time.

We Could Be Heroes

I push the Shit Machine into overdrive.

What I actually mean is I keep my foot to the floor at all times, regardless of road conditions or obstacles.

The engine whines like a bastard. I can hear the car sweating for me. Stench of engine oil and burning rubber. I'm killing a friend, but I don't have a choice.

I touch the brake periodically, just enough to slide me around corners or avoid pedestrians. Both screech in protest.

There's a traffic light. On red. I'm not going to wait for green and, besides, a queue of cars blocks my way. However, there is a pavement that's clear.

Well, relatively.

I turn the wheel a few degrees, drop into second, bounce over the kerb, hoping I don't take out the undercarriage, but what's left of it simply scrapes as it goes over. Foot off the brake, mash the accelerator and the car leaps forward again.

Go, Shit Machine!

I'm across the junction. Amazingly, no pedestrians or cars get in the way. One of those times everyone is waiting for everyone else. Or they heard me coming.

Even though I quite like being on the pavement, I decide that the road is a marginally better place.

Not far to go now. Fortunately.

There's smoke coming out of the bonnet and there's a knocking sound. Expiration appears imminent.

But there's the car park. Jerk to a stop. Konstantin and Lamb leap out. I pull away without waiting for the doors to close. Ten seconds driving, ninety degree turn. Even though the entrance is wide, I clip the wall, lose some speed and a bumper.

But that's okay, because multi-storeys are designed with economy of space in mind. Down to first and I'm heading up the switch back ramps to the roof.

Crash And Burn

There was a tap on the window, the harsh sound of metal on glass. Frank looked up.

One of Stevie's bodyguards was pointing a gun of his own. There was the other, Frank could see him through the front windscreen.

"Did you think I didn't know, Frank?" Stevie pressed the button on a car key fob. The boot popped and the ring tone was immediately louder. "You lyin' bastard. I suspected all along it was you. It just took me a little longer to track her down."

"What the fuck are you talking about?"

Stevie buzzed down the window, said, "One of you get her out. Show this thick bastard what's going on."

The guy out front disappeared, reappeared a few seconds later with Lucy. She was battered, bruised, gagged. Her hands were bound with plastic tie wraps. Frank's mouth fell open.

"That's what I'm talking about, old friend," Stevie said.

"What the fuck?"

"Hear that? It's the sound of me, still on top of the pile."

"But I don't know who she is."

"Yeah, yeah, Frank. Get out the car."

He complied. Looked at the girl, the two men either side of her. Stevie took the gun out of Frank's hand. He stepped out, nodded at the guy over the roof of the car. "Toss him. Then the copper." He turned to Frank. Said, "At least you'll have a nice sea view when you go."

Konstantin reached the roof. Knelt down and unclipped the case, then assembled the rifle. It was the work of moments to do so. He could literally slot the pieces together in his sleep. He fitted the scope, popped out the legs, rested them on the roof edge and knelt.

The Russian squinted through the lens, the car park roof jumped into view. But he immediately moved. The game might be in progress there, but it wasn't where the control emanated from. He scanned the other buildings, hoped he had enough time to tell Mr Lamb.

"I set up," he said into the mic.

"Okay, keep me appraised," he heard Mr Lamb reply in his ear. "We'll need to move fast."

"Don't we always?"

Konstantin shifted the lens back across the car park, stiffened when he caught a shock of blonde. Focused, saw Adam briefly, the pale scar he'd inflicted. He almost shot the man there and then, but knew he couldn't.

Instead, Konstantin let the events play their way and constantly swept the scope onto the adjoining buildings.

Stevie jerked in surprise as two gunshots rang out in heartbeat succession.

His bodyguards went down, hit the deck, didn't move. He looked at Lucy. She was splattered with their blood, an expression of shock carved on her face.

Adam stepped out from behind a pillar, pistol extended. Stevie swung his gun around. Frank pulled out his revolver and the three men stood in a triangle, shifting their aim from one to another.

Stalemate. Then all hell broke loose.

A lump of bent and battered metal on wheels emerged onto the top floor with a howl of pistons.

It flew off the ramp, a couple of feet in the air, landed with a bang of suspension on concrete. Squeal of tyres as it suddenly changed direction.

Stevie threw himself out of the way, flattened himself against the floor.

A wild volley of shots as Adam let loose half a clip. Stevie heard the crunch of metal then … silence. Moments later, a hubcap rolled across his line of sight.

Stevie pushed himself up and got to his feet, but stayed in a squat. Cautiously popped his head up.

This is what he saw:

The car was out of it. Steam vented from the bonnet.

It was pressed up against and into a Porsche (oddly, Stevie was pleased to see the poncy sports car smashed up).

The driver was obviously fucked.

As was Frank, who was squashed between the wrecked vehicles. Adam was out of sight.

Fuck knows where the girl was.

Stevie had no idea what to do next.

Konstantin saw the crash through the scope. He smiled, a very un-British action by a very British man. He relayed the activity to Mr Lamb over the headset.

Lucy glanced around, took in the scene of vehicular devastation, recognised the Shit Machine immediately through her hazy vision. Spots swam before her eyes.

She picked herself up, no easy task when your hands are bound together, weaved a little as she made her way to the car.

It hissed as the radiator leaked, water lazily turned to steam. She looked at Frank. He was spread-eagled over the bonnet, gun in hand.

Clearly dead.

David. She yanked the door open, pushed the reporter back in his seat. He flopped about like a rag doll, head rolled as far as it would go without falling off. His chest rose and fell shallowly.

Sleeping on the job. You lazy bastard.

Lucy put fingers on his neck. David's pulse was strong, regular. He'd survive, but with one monster of a headache. Maybe even concussion. He groaned then.

She stood up, looked around, wondered where her handler was in all this. He was supposed to be protecting her, ensuring this sort of shit didn't go down.

Then some primordial part of her brain detected movement, alerted her to danger. Lucy squinted, like a drunk trying to narrow her focus onto what was important to the exclusion of all else.

She took the gun from Frank's hand. He was warm to the touch. Wouldn't be for much longer. She heard a couple of quick steps, felt a barrel press against her head as she started to swing around.

"Do not move, pretty lady," she heard him say, saw David shift.

Revelation

I come to.

My skull is fucking pounding. My neck feels like it's stretched to breaking point. As my vision swims into focus, I can see the nicotine-stained vinyl roof of the Shit Machine. I tip my head forward. Very slowly.

It seems it takes an hour before I'm looking at myself in the rear-view mirror. There's a huge, red, crescent-shaped welt across my forehead. It's even dimpled with the pattern on the steering wheel. There's some blood too.

I look down the rest of my body. Seems okay, at first glance. I can't detect any gore or white bits of bone poking out. I have to shove at the door several times, because it's bent out of shape with the impact.

One of my ankles is compressed into a tight space where the engine has been pushed into where the pedals used to be. But it comes free with a bit of tugging and I'm out, on all fours, head down. Like an old dog that's just been dragged on far too long a walk.

I lean against the Shit Machine for support, momentarily. There's Frank to my left. He's slumped over the bonnet, his face is pressed into the dented metal, arms splayed in surrender.

I remember aiming for him. Good shot. Makes the expiration of my metal friend almost worth it.

Push off the car and stagger around a bit. One leg feels like it's shorter than the other.

"Excellent driving," someone says.

I recognise him. Adam, the blonde guy with the scarred face. He's standing behind Lucy, gun at her temple. She looks remarkably calm, twitches an eyebrow at me in a laconic greeting.

"Well, isn't this wonderful?" Another voice. Stevie the Steroid, also armed. I feel left out. "The reporter, the terrorist and the copper."

"A copper?"

"Yes, didn't you know?" He sees my expression. "Oh, you fucking moron. She's undercover. Been playing you like a violin."

I look at Lucy to see if Stevie is lying. He's not. Her face is hard, emotionless. My heart sinks. She glares at Oakhill.

"Well done for taking out Frank, by the way," Stevie continues. "Saved me the job."

"You're welcome." I sound beaten, even to myself.

A phone rings. It's mine. Stops. Rings again.

"Answer it," Stevie says.

I do. "Put me on speaker," the voice says.

"Meadows, you bastard," Stevie says.

There's a chuckle down the phone.

"What the fuck is going on?" Adam asks.

He still has his gun to Lucy's temple.

"We've all been set up," Stevie says.

A shot rings out.

I See You

"I see him," Konstantin said.

"Where?" Mr Lamb replied. "Tell me where."

Konstantin described the building, heard Mr Lamb take off at a run. He swung the scope back onto the car park. Meadows wasn't his problem now.

End Game

Adam is down. The projectile went straight through his skull. I doubt he even knew what hit him. His eyes are wide, vacant. Blood is already pooling where he lies.

I hear a chuckle over the speaker. "Oops! Sorry, Adam. Slippery trigger-finger."

The guy is clearly off his head.

"Lucy," he says. She hasn't moved a millimetre. "Pick up his gun, Lucy. No sudden movements, Stevie. You saw what happened to the Chechen. Go on, Lucy, you've got your nemesis right in front of you. It's what you've been waiting for. Pick up the gun. For Andrew."

She pauses a moment, then does as he says. Snatches the weapon from the floor, raises it until the barrel is aiming dead centre at Stevie's forehead. He doesn't give a shit, just grins at her.

I say, "Don't do it, Lucy."

"It doesn't matter, Mr Reporter," says Stevie. "There's no way any of us are getting off this roof alive. Isn't that so, Meadows?"

He receives another chuckle in reply.

"You killed my brother!" Lucy shouted at Oakhill.

"I've no idea who you are, love, so I cannot confirm or deny your accusation." The wind ruffles our clothes, but no-one feels the chill.

"Andrew Ryan. He worked for one of Dredge's companies. He was my twin. You killed him!"

It hits me then. The guy on Mrs Ryan's wall in the funereal picture frame.

Oakhill shrugs. "People die every day."

I can see Lucy tightening her finger on the trigger.

"Do it then, darling," Oakhill says. "Kill me. Take revenge for your little brother."

"Andrew was older than me. By four minutes."

He sneers. Says, "He's dead. He'll be younger than you forever."

She seems to lose the energy then. Like the gun is too heavy to hold. It sags.

"If you point a shooter at someone, love, you've got to be prepared to finish it," Oakhill says. "I know I am."

Oakhill raises his own firearm and in a fluid movement pulls the trigger.

Lucy doesn't move. Oakhill, though, stares open mouthed. Red blooms across his chest. He looks down at the wound, sags to his knees and, a moment later, keels onto his side. I run to Lucy, pull her down onto the floor, hopefully out of sight of the rifle.

My phone rings.

"Get out of there," Mr Lamb says. "We've got you covered."

I disconnect, tell Lucy to come on. She doesn't move. I bodily pull her up. She's compliant, flexible like a rag doll.

I tug the gun out of her hands, throw it away, then hustle her to the steps.

We take them as quickly as we can, but still far too slowly.

Then we're on the ground floor and out into the sunlight. Konstantin is waiting for us, case in hand, huge smile on his face. Says, "We need go, before police arrive."

Misfire

Meadows couldn't understand it. He'd checked the wiring himself. Yet, when he'd depressed the button, the car bombs hadn't been triggered. Which was a slight problem, because the witnesses were still alive. But still, not a tragedy.

Meadows congratulated himself on an otherwise flawless plan as he got into his car. Started the drive to Manston, only a handful of miles away, where a private jet awaited him.

Home free.

Mr Lamb followed the copper at a measured distance. Knew where Meadows was heading. But not who he was going to meet.

Epilogue
The Spider's Webs

Today

There's not much more to say.

Just couple of extra paragraphs.

I down a whiskey, finish a fag that I swear is my last, stub it out, light another.

I apply my aching fingers to the keys …

We get a taxi to the train station. Neither of us says a word the whole journey. I hold her in my arms. She shakes the whole while.

I put her on the train to London. From there, she can go anywhere she wants.

She kisses me lightly on the lips, puts a soft hand to my cheek, then steps inside the carriage.

As the train pulls away, I feel someone at my side. He flashes a badge I barely see.

Re-introduces himself. DCI Troon, the hard-faced Scot. Transpires he's Internal Affairs.

Over a shitty coffee in the station café, he gives me a five minute rundown. I don't know why, he owes me nothing. Says it's a favour for Lamb. Whatever.

Troon tells me I'm lucky not to be going to jail.

I shrug, say there's nothing more to take away from me.

James Hollowman. Was a whistle-blower, ready to take the lid off before he was killed, believed to have been ordered by Oakhill, carried out by Frank.

Meadows. Another bent cop in a long line of bent cops. Had been under Oakhill's wing for years, taking kickbacks in exchange for information. But he'd begun to chafe, wanted out and needed his money to pay off debts, so he hatched a plot to do both. Little had he known he was being watched himself. Killed Culpepper, made it look like suicide, probably because he'd been sniffing around Meadows' account and tripped an alert.

Frank. Was a snitch. Meadows was using him to take down Stevie with the promise of taking over the gang, but that was never going to happen. No way would Meadows swap one master for another. So he was always going to wind up dead.

Adam. The Chechen terrorist was involved by pure chance. He really had been muscling in on Oakhill, so Meadows used this to his advantage. Fed the guy information whilst telling Stevie he was holding Adam off.

Lucy. She'd had a breakdown a year ago. Tried to kill herself. Prior to that, she'd been a highly promising undercover cop on Meadows' task force. But afterwards, was a wreck. Living proof that twins can't bear to be separated from their other half, particularly in traumatic circumstances. Lucy had returned home on sick leave, once she'd been released. Meadows brought her back into the game to go after Oakhill. Back-up really. In case all else failed.

I ask where Meadows is.

Troon says they're letting him run.

Sprat to catch a mackerel. Bigger tactics in play.

I almost smack him one there and then.

Get up and leave without another word. He can pay for the drinks.

Retrieve my laptop, go home and don't stop writing.

I want to blow this shitty story wide open.

I'm knackered, but I've never felt better in my life. Keep typing …

There's a knock. Then another. I have to hurry. Nearly finished.

But he doesn't wait for me. The front door to my house is kicked off its hinges by the size twelve boots of the Russian tramp with an odour to die for.

There's dust in the air, wood splinters on the floor.

Konstantin just grins at me. A 'gotcha' kind of look.

He walks over, footfalls surprisingly quiet for such a big guy. Looms over my shoulder. Reads these words, like you.

"You not quite done," he says.

"Well, I kind of got fucking interrupted," comes my reply.

Konstantin laughs, a big boom that bounces off the walls, like we're in a cave.

"So, type," the Russian rasps, quiet-like, grit in my ear.

As you know, I always grab an opportunity with both hands. Rattle away.

He looks at my final words.

"Send it," he says.

Open an e-mail to my editor.

Final click of the mouse.

All hell breaks loose.

The Fix

The first Konstantin novel by Keith Nixon is available in paperback and eBook from all good book shops and online.

Paperback £8.99
eBook from £1.99

Russian Roulette

Konstantin is back in a series of short stories unveiling a little of the mysteries of the genesis of the man.

Paperback £8.99
eBook from £1.99

Lightning Source UK Ltd.
Milton Keynes UK
UKOW02f0655060515

250955UK00002BA/38/P